Gomorrah

Gomorrah

MARVIN KARLINS

and

LEWIS M. ANDREWS

DOUBLEDAY & COMPANY, INC.

GARDEN CITY, NEW YORK

1974

To Terri Hesse—my Wharton whiz

—M.K.

Library of Congress Cataloging in Publication Data

Karlins, Marvin.
Gomorrah.

I. Andrews, Lewis M., joint author. II. Title.
PZ4.K1767Go [PS3561.A63]   813'.5'4
ISBN 0-385-02096-1
Library of Congress Catalog Card Number 74-1503

CHAPTER ONE

Hell's Gauntlet they had called it. Back in the seventies when Victor was in college, before URDEC. Victor had run the gauntlet once, in an old Penn Central coach with tired windows and stained seats. It had been crushingly hot that day, and as he rode the elevated train between row after row of crumbling stone buildings Victor could see scores of people hanging out of windows like ruptured flour sacks, their breath spilling into the sulfurous haze that New Yorkers called "air."

"Maybe it's too hot for trouble today," one of the conductors had told a passenger as the train pulled out of the 125th Street station. "Don't count on it," the passenger had replied, squinting out the window until the sallow faces in the crippled buildings merged into one wretched tapestry, "those niggers come from the jungle, you know."

The conductor had nodded and opened his mouth to speak when the first stone struck, a resounding metallic report that sent the passengers scrambling away from the few remaining unboarded window seats. Victor had been startled at first, a momentary feeling of uncertainty quickly replaced by a surge of excitement as volley after volley of rocks bounded off the car's metal superstructure. Most of the stones produced more noise than damage, but before the siege was over the outside panes of two safety windows had been shattered.

Now it was fifteen years later and Victor Slaughter was

running the gauntlet again, but this time his train coach was armor plated, and the projectiles rattling off its sides were bullets, not stones. Riding atop the coach in the small observation dome housing the ARC gun, Victor watched as a burst of tracer bullets blossomed from the darkness of a shattered brownstone, vivid orange tendrils that brushed by the curved steelglas above his seat. The ARC gunner pivoted his weapon thirty degrees and returned the fire, sending yellow concussion modules spinning and tumbling crazily along the ragged sidewalks and rubble heaps. The firefight had a surreal quality: the bubble-topped, two-car train moving like some grotesque mechanical camel between jagged cliffs of gutted buildings, the hum of the Automatic Riot Control gun as it pressurized the concussion modules, the vivid orange and yellow probes, all set against the backdrop of mid-Manhattan's hulking skyline.

The exchange of gunfire continued sporadically until the train dipped into the access tunnel that curled around Grand Central Station and into Oasis One. "Quiet night," observed the gunner, slipping out of his harness.

"Quiet?" Victor swiveled his chair around so that he could face the gunner directly.

"Quiet," the gunner repeated. "Last month we almost caught a mortar round above 160th." He placed the harness over the back of his chair and swung out of the turret. "Things are getting better, though, since O.C. gave us permission to set the modules at kill pressure."

"O.C.?"

"Oasis Command." The gunner gave Victor a cursory glance. "You're new to the city, aren't you?"

Victor ignored the question. "What did you do before that?"

"Not much we could do," the gunner grunted, tugging

at the master power lever beside the aft-gun compression chamber. "We used a four-plus impact setting—knocked the Dregs fifteen feet into their ratholes, but they'd be back the next day for more." The gunner waited until power shutoff was complete before he jacketed the gun's muzzle. "You *are* new to the city, aren't you?"

"I was here for a summer once . . . but a while back." Victor pivoted his chair gently to keep the gunner in view. "Last time I rode this line it was one of those electric jobs on wires."

The gunner stretched and walked over to the chair across from Victor. "Whew," he said, sprawling heavily into the chair and letting out his breath in a low whistle, "that *was* a long time ago. Those cars were death traps. One snip of the power lines and the Dregs had 'em like sitting ducks. These babies have their own power now. Let me ask you something," the gunner requested, taking a pack of cigarettes from his pocket. "Smoke?"

"No, thanks. What?"

"Why are you riding this train?"

Victor gave the gunner an inquisitive look.

"I mean, why not fly to New York?"

"Oh, I see," Victor nodded. "I had to get in this evening, and there were no flights out of Albany until tomorrow morning."

"Uh-huh." The gunner tapped the cigarette against his thumbnail. "I figured something like that."

"You did?"

"Yup," he said, reaching into his pocket for a lighter. "This isn't exactly a pleasure trip. At least the planes fly over all this crap." The gunner lit his cigarette, the flame plainly visible in the low illumination of the dome. "You with the state?"

Victor shook his head. "Insurance. One of the Manhattan office buildings we cover was bombed today."

"So, what's new?" The gunner took a long drag on his cigarette, exhaling the smoke slowly in two columns from his nose. "I thought you might be working on the kidnapping."

"The Stenley woman?"

"Yeah . . . there were five men from the front car up here earlier. Reporters covering the case. And there's two FBI men in this car—seems everyone on the train has something to do with it."

Victor shrugged. "Seems like a hell of a lot of people spending a hell of a lot of time looking for one missing person."

"And a scummer at that," the gunner added. "I'll tell you, I wouldn't mind if they found her . . . dead."

"I gather you don't think much of her ideas."

"Ideas? You call *those* ideas?" The gunner took another long drag on his cigarette and crushed it, hardly smoked, into an ashtray next to his chair. "Trash. She spoke garbage. Can you believe it—she wanted to arm the Dregs!"

"I thought she just wanted to guarantee their protection from—"

"Same thing," the gunner interrupted angrily. "Those bastards are running the streets like mad dogs already . . . robbing, killing, blowing up your damn buildings . . . and this scummer wants to give *them* protection. . . ."

"But—"

"No buts! The woman is dangerous. Why didn't she stay in Washington . . . we didn't ask her to come."

"No, I guess you have a point there," Victor agreed.

"You bet I do," the gunner retorted, with a little less bluster. "Sometimes people like you—you know, people who don't *live* in the city—just can't appreciate the problem."

"You're right there, too, I guess. Although I was here in the past."

"It's not the same today. We're coming in now, you'll see for yourself."

Now that his attention had been called to it, Victor could feel the train braking to a stop. Outside the dome, the tunnel walls gave way to a brightly lighted platform and he could see the small bulletproof electrocars used for transportation in Oasis One. The gunner got up from his seat just as the train shuddered to a halt against the restraining coil at the mouth of the platform. He moved directly to the exit stairs, but before he started his descent he paused and turned toward Victor. "I've got two more months on this job and then I'm getting the hell out. This city is dying and I'll be damned if I'm going to die with it."

"But how can you be so sure it's dying?" Victor asked, motioning the gunner to wait.

The gunner moved down the stairs and out of the train without answering his question.

CHAPTER TWO

Oasis Entry was an old midtown Seventh Avenue subway station that had been transformed into an armed fortress. Victor was well apprised of developments in New York since his summer visit, yet even he was momentarily stunned when he stepped from the train and actually confronted the enormity of the changes he had been briefed about. If Oasis Entry was an indication of things to come, then Victor was entering a city on the edge of siege. Everywhere a crisp sense of military readiness prevailed. On the ground, man and machine moved smartly to a martial cadence, the stop-and-go rhythm of checkpoints and convoys. In the air, steelglas surveillance globes glided like crystal spiders along silver wiretracks, watching and listening. Along the walls, ARC gun barrels protruded from remotely controlled ball turrets, the muzzles sweeping smoothly through 180-degree arcs. The whole underground chamber was not unlike the subsurface missile silos Victor had visited during his training—right down to the Rillium surface plating and atmosphere-support units. Yet there was a difference. Military personnel frequently moved around missile bases with grim, tight expressions on their faces. In Oasis One, however, the police guards sported uniformly manicured smiles. It was as if their expressions had been poured from the same mold. They probably had been, Victor thought. He was familiar with the Oasis edict that required all security personnel to act polite and cheerful in the presence of visitors.

"Your papers, please." The voice came from behind Victor's left shoulder. He turned to confront an Entry guard, his hand outstretched.

"Here you are," Victor said, extracting his identiplate and travelpas from his billfold.

The guard studied the two plastic microcards for several moments before responding. "You're logged into Oasis Control," he finally noted, somewhat confused. "Insurance claims agent . . . ?"

"I need to take a deposition at Police Central," Victor explained.

"I see." The guard handed Victor his travelpas. "You know that'll require VP clearance."

"Yes."

"Fine. Would you please step over to the identification cubicles." The guard pointed past a cluster of electrocars and baggage-inspection stations to a row of refurbished phone booths where the computer terminals had been installed.

Victor complied, picking up his suitcase and following the guard to the first vacant terminal.

"In here, please," the guard instructed, pointing to the stool fronting the computer equipment. "We'll take the voice print as soon as I feed in your credentials." The Entry officer placed Victor's identiplate on the intake slot of the terminal and jiggled it until it slid out of sight. There was a soft humming sound and the green ready light appeared above the speaker grid. Victor repeated his name three times. Then, in a matter of seconds, the identiplate and a blue confirmation decal slid out of the machine and into the officer's waiting hand, and the typing element on the central communicator began tattooing its clearance visa across the unfolding sheets of printout paper. The officer gave a perfunctory glance at the coded information and handed Victor back his identiplate. "Thank you for your patience," he said, the manufactured smile reappearing on his lips. "Now let's get you to your destination."

Victor followed his escort out of the terminal area—past the visitor entry docket with its rows of gleaming airtrains, down a winding corridor that seemed to run on for blocks, and finally into a semicircular enclosure that served as the embarcation platform for people with assigned carriers. Victor didn't have to wait long for his transportation—a chauffered electrocar—to arrive. The guard had barely logged in their arrival when it rolled up to the loading zone. "Have you ever been to Police Central before?" the guard wanted to know.

"Never."

"Nothing to worry about," the guard said, pushing the door-activation button on the vehicle's roof, "all the information you'll need is videophone recorded inside." The door panel slid open and Victor eased himself onto the gray vinyl seat behind the driver's partition. The door slid silently shut behind him. Looking out his steelglas window, Victor could see the guard placing the confirmation decal over the door and activating it. It was the last thing he saw before the driver swung the car away from the lighted platform and into the semidarkness of the Oasis roadway.

"May I have a word with you, please." The compelling voice captured Victor's attention and he looked up to confront an attractive, middle-aged woman speaking from the transport's domespot videophone. She was seated at a table, holding a large metal key aloft, and smiling broadly. Next to her a huge man in a tan Oasis police security blazer looked on attentively while, behind him, the words HELLO VISITOR were scrawled in lights across an autocom panel.

"Welcome to New York City," the woman said cheerily, pushing the key in Victor's direction. "All of us here at Oasis One wish you a pleasant stay and stand ready to help you unlock the treasures of our community."

Victor winced.

The woman put the key on the table and picked up a scale model of Victor's transport. "For your convenience and safety we have provided you with a ride to your destination." She pointed to the model while the autocom panel flashed THERE IS NO CHARGE FOR THIS SERVICE on and off. "While you are en route please sit back, relax, and enjoy the ride. And now," the woman turned to her male colleague, "I'd like to introduce you to Captain Steven Anderson, Director of Internal Security for Oasis One. Captain . . ."

Captain Anderson nodded and leaned forward in his chair, the manicured Oasis smile frozen onto his lips. Behind him the autocom panel traced out a police badge with the departmental motto prominently displayed in blinking colored lights. SAFETY AND SECURITY WITH A SMILE. SAFETY AND SECURITY WITH A SMILE. SAFETY AND SECURITY WITH A SMILE. "In a few minutes," the captain began, "you'll be arriving at your destination refreshed, relaxed, and safe. Isn't it nice to know that while you visit or do business in Oasis One you can do so in complete peace of mind—secure in the knowledge that our Oasis is the safest urban complex in the world. Did you know, for instance, that we have the lowest rate of violent crimes anywhere? *Anywhere*," Anderson repeated, as the autocom panel lighted up a dazzling array of crime statistics. Anderson thrust his face closer to the TV camera. "We like that record and want to keep it intact. Therefore, we ask your cooperation in observing a few simple rules created for your comfort and safety."

Captain Anderson pushed back his chair and stood up. "Do not . . ." he said, walking around the table and sitting on the front edge, "do not leave your carrier while it is taking you to your destination. If you do you'll break the confirmation decal over the door and trigger an alarm to traffic control. You will be subject to a fine and detention for an ID update if you break a confirmation decal. If an emergency should arise and you need immediate assistance, pick up the videophone, state your problem, and help will be dispatched. Don't try to solicit aid from your driver—he cannot hear you through the steelglas partition."

The captain reached over and picked the metal key off the table, balancing it between his two forefingers. "Don't loiter near Oasis perimeters or wander into the redzones next to the steelglas parapets. Keep your identiplate and travelpas with you at all times. If you should lose either, report this to the police at once. Do not tamper with surveillance modules, they are there for your protection. And, finally, in the rare case of an Oasis emergency, please follow the instructions you will hear broadcast over the public-address monitors. You know," Anderson said, shifting the key between his thumb and forefinger and scrutinizing it carefully, "safety is the key to our city. Remember this. . . ." The captain gestured toward the autocom panel, which burst into full illumination with a ten-thousand-watt re-creation of the New York skyline. Above the buildings a glowing banner announced WELCOME TO FUN CITY—LET'S KEEP IT THAT WAY.

Victor shook his head as the video image faded. "Only

in New York," he mused, leaning back and watching as the roadway widened and his transport was joined by an influx of electrocars gliding effortlessly nearby, their box-like bodies glowing like phosphorescent cubes in the darkness. Then his transport veered off from the main traffic pattern and onto the intake ramp for Oasis Central. A slight bump told Victor that his vehicle had mounted the final inspection checkpoint at the mouth of the ramp. For fifteen seconds his transport moved along the grooved causeway as a traffic computer cleared him for entry status; then there was a second bump, a sharp upgrade, and suddenly Victor's carrier spilled over the rim of the ramp and into the cavernous garage serving Oasis Central.

It was almost 1 A.M., yet the underground complex was far from quiet. Traffic moved everywhere: a shimmering mosaic of trucks, cars, and heavy machinery bathed in the daylight brilliance of sodium arc lights. It was obvious that New York's largest remaining nerve center was pulsating with vigorous life. If the city was dying, as the train gunner had suggested, the crush of people in Oasis Central hadn't gotten the message. Transport vehicles were lined up twenty deep to bring passengers into the headquarter complex, and by the time Victor reached the entry checkpoint, twice that number seemed to stretch out behind him along the arrival concourse.

Considering the volume of traffic moving through the Oasis checkpoint, Victor's entry clearance proceeded with a minimum of delay. Handed an identification badge and Police Central map, he made his way past guardpoints and a maze of corridors and ramps until he reached a sign marked POLICE DEPARTMENT: FOURTH DIVISION. Directly under the sign, a desk sergeant was thumbing through a newspaper. He acknowledged Victor's presence with a cursory glance and returned to his reading.

Victor was surprised by the lax attitude of the sergeant. After the precision security checks throughout his trip, it seemed so out of place. He fingered his identification badge and cleared his throat sharply.

The sergeant looked up again, his face clearly showing annoyance, and asked, "What do you want?"

"If possible . . ." Victor reached for his travelpas and held it out for the sergeant, "I want to see Officer Marba."

The sergeant ignored the travelpas. "Marba's office is down to the end of the hall and the last office on the right."

"Down the hall . . . last office on the right," Victor repeated, pointing out directions as he spoke. "May I take my suitcase?"

"Be my guest," the sergeant answered, turning back to his newspaper.

Victor picked up his bag and started down the long corridor. Although Police Central was one of the most impressive and handsomely furnished departments in the Oasis Central complex, one wouldn't have guessed it by observing the peeling plaster and battered furniture in the Records Section of the Fourth Division. No wonder it was nicknamed "The Graveyard"—a place where washed-up cops were kept busy and out of the way sorting documents and retrieving microfilms until their retirement day, when they were quickly hustled out of the force with no pomp and little pension. Victor lowered his eyes. It certainly wasn't the place for a Psycor founder to be working.

The last office on the right turned out to be a builder's afterthought—a stuffy little cubicle squeezed between the fire escape and the janitor's closet; such a small, tight space between the pressing walls, it seemed ready to pop out like an air blister between two stone slabs. The door to the office was ajar. It was a warped and rotting plywood affair, the wood grain showing where the dark-stain finish had rubbed away. A frosted pane, inlaid with chickenwire, rested loosely in the door's upper frame. One segment of the glass, where names were painted on and scraped off, had been worn down to the wire mesh. There was no name on the door now.

Victor peered inside. There were only four pieces of aged wooden furniture within the tiny roomcell, and they merely added to the ramshackle, coffinlike atmosphere that permeated the place. A long table leaned wearily against one wall like a heavily laden old mare, its back bent and legs sagging under the weight of neatly stacked papers. A broken chair with two cracked backslats and a wobbled leg rested against the crippled table. A mate to the broken chair and a rolltop desk, both creaky-ancient, faced away from the door, toward the far wall. The room was dimly lighted by a desklamp on the rolltop and a grime-encrusted bulb hanging from the ceiling by a braided cord. A man was seated at the rolltop, surrounded by orderly piles of manila file folders.

"Lieutenant Marba?"

The man turned in his chair and studied Victor with an unwavering gaze. For a moment Victor said nothing. He returned Marba's gaze, trying to fathom how the years could change a man so much. The eyes had been spared —they were still clear and alert, steel-blue beaconpoints, searching, seeing. But the rest of Marba's face: the lean, proud line of the chin; the clear, smooth skin stretched taut over the high cheekbones; the shock of sandy brown hair tumbling over the fine, broad forehead—what had

happened to it? The face confronting Victor was puffy
and lined, the skin loose and tinged with red blotches—it
was an *old* face, worn and cracked like the furniture
around it. Victor's hand reflexively brushed over the contours of his own face.

"Yes?"

In the brief moment it took Marba to make his inquiry,
Victor had regained his composure. But that was too
long for a man trained to conceal his emotional responses.
He cursed himself for the mental lapse and wondered if
Marba had detected his loss of self-control. "I'm Vic
Slaughter," Victor said. "May I come in?"

"I know who you are, and I know what you want,"
Marba snapped. "And I can do without being gaped at,"
he added tersely.

"I'm sorry, it's just that . . ."

"That what . . . ?"

"Well, that you don't look like your picture at the
academy."

Marba snorted. "I guess that's justice of a sort. The
academy doesn't exactly conform to the image I created
for it, either."

"Sir?"

"Hell, forget it—you wouldn't understand. Come in and
let's get this over with so I can get back to some important work."

Victor shrugged off the old man's comments and
stepped into the room. He had been forewarned about
Marba's hostile attitude and he wasn't about to let an
elderly sorehead get his goat—particularly after his emo-
tive faux pas of a few moments ago. Picking up the
broken chair, he carried it over to Marba and gingerly sat
down.

"I'll get right to the point," Marba said flatly, beginning to speak even before his visitor was seated. "I didn't ask for any help on this case and frankly I don't need any. Particularly your kind of help."

"I assure you I am competent at my job," Victor protested. "I—"

"Your job is violence," Marba interrupted, ". . . and I can solve this kidnapping without more damn killing."

"My job is to be a competent Psycor agent, which I am," Victor retorted in a steady, measured voice. "For someone who helped found Psycor and teach most of the first operatives, you should appreciate my value."

"If only it were so!" Marba leaned forward until his face was only a few inches from Victor's. "In the old days Psycor agents did have value—and they had *values* as well. A sense of dignity and humanity. Did you know that's why we created Psycor in the first place: to train a group of agents who could do the job, but do it with compassion for human life. Compassion . . ." Marba repeated, his eyes fixed on Victor's face, "not murder and mayhem."

"And this is what your compassion got you . . . an office down here?" Victor observed, unable to pass up the opportunity to deflate his pompous heckler.

The red went out of Marba's face and he got up abruptly, almost knocking over his chair. "I'll tell you what got me down here," he said angrily, "standing up for my ideals. But you wouldn't understand that, would you. All you understand is numbed minds and dead bodies." Marba stepped back, his eyes widening. "Don't you think I can't get you off this case—I'm still in charge of eastern operations, and you'll do as I say or you'll get the fuck outa here."

Victor had hit a raw nerve and it gave him satisfaction to see Marba squirm. If it hadn't been for the old man's seniority and stubborn insistence that he be in command, Victor probably would have received the Stenley assignment and solved it already. Besides, as he had argued to Central Operations, what the hell was a retirement-age deskman trying to prove going out to direct such a vital field assignment. Logistically it was a washout—but Victor hadn't been able to convince his superiors of that, and he wasn't about to convince Marba, either.

"I'm sure you can replace me," Victor replied to Marba, deciding that further conflict with his enraged superior would get him nowhere. "But there's no guarantee the replacement will be any better. Look, I don't agree one bit with your assessment of me or my colleagues, but if we're going to have to work together, why don't we act like professionals and forget our personal differences."

Victor's conciliatory gesture seemed to have a calming effect on Marba. He paced up and down for several moments, but when he finally spoke his tone was noticeably subdued. "All right . . . but you'll take your orders from me and do as I say. Is that understood?"

"Yes," Victor agreed, "as long as I'm involved in the case all the way."

"Yeah . . . okay," Marba grunted, "but keep in line. Nobody—not you, not the police department, not even Psycor is going to mess up my efforts to solve this kidnapping." Marba returned to his seat and leaned back heavily in his ramshackle chair. "There's too much riding on this case to botch it," he explained in almost reverent tones, ". . . too much riding on it. . . ."

"What? Why is this case so important to you?"

"Because the Stenley woman can help save this city."

"Why would anyone want to save New York?" Victor asked, half in jest.

Marba said nothing but Victor could tell that he was

thinking. The clear blue eyes had ceased to focus and were wandering dreamily in their sockets. When he finally did speak it was in a faraway voice. "You didn't grow up in the city . . . you don't know what it feels like to have New York in your blood. And you can't appreciate how it feels to see the city torn apart . . . piece by piece."

"It looks like it's doing quite well now."

"Where? Here in the Oasis?"

"Yes—it isn't exactly a ghost town."

Marba shook his head sadly. "Oasis One is not New York City. It is what its name implies: a tiny spot of lushness surrounded by desolation. It is crowded because almost all New York visitors stay here. It is active because most of New York's remaining business is conducted here. Remember that the Oasis was built as a fortress against crime—a place where travelers and businessmen could go about their affairs conveniently and safely. It still serves that function. But outside the parapets, beyond the redzones, there's a wasteland out there. A rotting wasteland filled with crumbling buildings and broken people. A world crammed with junkies, perverts, beggars, cripples —the 'dregs' of society."

"And the middle class citizens . . . where do they live?"

"Those who haven't already left the city or found living quarters in the Oasis or the secured zones . . . they're out there, too. Heavily armed and very frightened."

"And probably very desperate," Victor predicted.

"Extremely. You have to see it to believe it. The fear, I mean. They've learned to survive with it—but their faces . . . it's there, stamped into their faces."

"I'd like to see those faces," Victor suggested, checking his watch. "Can we see a bit of the city before the briefing?"

Marba looked surprised. "I didn't think you'd be interested," he observed skeptically.

"I want to see if it's as bad as you say. How about it? The meeting's at eight o'clock—can you pick me up outside the Hilton at, say, six-thirty?"

Marba thought for a moment and nodded. "All right. Just remember what I said about following orders."

"And remember what I said about being competent," Victor replied, getting up and moving toward the door.

"Not so fast." Marba took a thick manila envelope from the top of his desk and tossed it to Victor. "That's the updated Stenley file . . . know it cold by the time I pick you up."

"But that's less than five hours away."

Marba clasped his hands teepee style under his chin, a smug expression on his face. "I'm just remembering what you said about your competence. I'm sure *you* won't have any difficulty getting the job done."

Victor started to protest, but thought better of it. He put the bulging envelope under his arm, picked up his suitcase, and opened the door to go.

"And, Mr. Slaughter, I . . . uh . . . just want you to know that even though I may look a bit out of shape, I have this case under control."

"I'm sure you do," Victor said, pausing in the entryway to give Marba an attentive look. Then he stepped into the hall and shut the door firmly behind him.

CHAPTER THREE

Out beyond the parapets, away from the color and clamor of Oasis One, there was only an overwhelming sense of gray: the drab gray of a pallored city staggering to wakefulness, its stained and weary buildings blending into the first light of an overcast morning. For a while Marba drove Victor around the city in silence, letting the grayness sink in. Outwardly the city hadn't changed that much since Victor's summer visit. The number of rundown and bruised buildings had certainly increased, but, driving through the areas of New York he knew best, Victor was impressed by how familiar they appeared. Yet the city *was* different. "I get a different feeling," he explained, speaking to Marba for the first time since leaving the Oasis.

Marba shrugged.

"I mean, it doesn't *feel* like New York."

"You mean it doesn't *breathe* like New York," Marba corrected. "You notice how quiet it is?"

"It's early."

"Going on seven o'clock," the lieutenant agreed. "But was it ever this quiet at seven o'clock when you were around?"

"Not this quiet."

"Or this deserted," Marba added. "Look . . . there on your left."

Victor glanced sideways at a row of tenements extending the length of the block.

"They were all abandoned in the past five years."

"Nobody lives there?"

"Nobody but the Dregs—and maybe a few runaways."

"But . . . they don't look so bad from the outside."

"Structurally, there's nothing wrong with them."

"Then why . . . ?"

"The residents either left the city or moved to a safer area."

Victor pointed to the next cross street, where additional tenements were crushed together along both sides of the narrow roadway. "The same down there?"

"Yes, and the same in a lot of other places—particularly the upper West Side."

"I know . . . I came in that way."

"You know . . ." Marba exhaled sharply. "How much do you know?"

"What is that supposed to mean?"

"How much can you really appreciate the changes that've taken place since your summer vacation?"

"You been on that Penn Central excuse for a tank recently?"

"That—"

"Or through the human dissection they call a 'VP clearance' at Oasis Entry?"

Marba reached into his shirt pocket and glanced at a small black notebook. "What you're referring to are surface impressions . . . blemishes on the skin of the city. The real changes are down deeper—here, where the city is hollow; where they took the heart out. Here, where New York doesn't breathe anymore."

"They . . . ?"

"Listen . . . we have time before the briefing . . . I'm

going to show you what a town with consumption really
looks like." Marba eased his car onto an almost deserted
Twenty-second Street and headed toward the West Side
Highway.

"That's a police logbook, isn't it?" Victor inquired,
pointing to the notebook in Marba's shirt pocket.

"Yes."

"Wonder what could be in there you'd want me to
see?"

"You'll find out . . . just sit tight," Marba suggested,
staring out his windshield at the almost traffic-free roadway. In less than fifteen minutes he had reached his
destination: a long line of police barricades cordoning off
Broadway at Ninety-sixth Street.

"What now . . . and why all the people?" Victor asked,
pointing toward the row of wooden obstructions and the
knots of people crowded behind them. "That's more people than I've seen the entire morning."

"I'll find a parking place and we'll join them." Marba
hung a wide U-turn and pulled his unmarked patrol car
into a truck-loading zone.

"The people don't seem very afraid of each other," Victor observed, getting out of the car and locking the door
behind him.

"They're about as safe as they'll ever be standing next
to a bunch of strangers in New York. You see," Marba
gestured, pointing to a small opening behind one of the
barricades, "during a dogging there's a kind of unwritten
truce between the cops and the citizens, and among the
citizens themselves."

"A *dogging?*"

"A dogging—move in here and you'll see one for yourself."

Victor pushed in sideways next to his companion, who

had edged to the front of the line and was standing, feet spread wide, to gain as much space for himself as possible. "You're a policeman, why can't we cross the line?" Victor asked.

"This is a special detail—only cops assigned to the dogging unit can participate."

"Then how do those people rate?" Victor asked, pointing to a cluster of individuals standing inside the police cordon.

"They aren't people, they're tourists," Marba said in disgust. "Their tour package guarantees them special sight lines—for a price."

"Seems sensible to me. I can't see that well from here."

"They're sick," Marba argued, an ugly scowl crossing his face. "Fuckin' vultures paying a price to see the city die. They come up here from all over—I hear 'em on the street whispering about the crime and how frightened they are—and all the while they can't wait to lay down their money and see a dogging or take a crime tour and maybe, if they're lucky, see a mugging or watch a rape."

"Not exactly a Grey Line tour down the Great White Way."

"I wish there was a Broadway left." Marba leaned his weight against the wooden barrier in front of him and gazed stonily ahead. "Frankly, I wish one of those tour buses would get knocked over . . . give those fuckers a real ride for their money. A *real* ride for their money," he repeated, a flatness in his voice.

Victor turned to confront Marba with another question but he never got the chance to ask it. "Here they come!" somebody shouted from nearby, and the next thing he knew a crush of people were jamming against him, pushing his body sharply into the teetering wooden barricade. "What the hell," he said to no one in particular, a bit incensed over the rudeness of the crowd. Marba seemed unaffected by the whole thing. He kept staring ahead, his massive body planted firmly against the thrusts of the latecomers jostling up from behind. "Give those fuckers a real ride for their money," he said again, his voice barely audible over the growing din around him.

"Get back! Get back!" From the eastern end of the block two policemen on horseback moved rapidly along the line of barricades, using their mounts to drive people up on the sidewalks. Then, above the shouts of the officers and the noise of the crowd, Victor heard it for the first time: muffled and far off but unmistakable, the sound of dogs barking and yelping. The sound of the animals seemed to trigger the crowd into a state of frenzy. There was no restraint: people began to jump up and down, their arms and legs flailing, their eyes sprung wide in their sockets, their mouths gulping in air and letting out shrieks and grunts. And above it all, like some swelling cacophony of terror, the howling dogs coming inexorably closer. It was not until Victor actually caught sight of the dogs that he became aware of a second sound: the roar of motors at full throttle. Then all the sounds seemed to blend into one terrible, explosive tapestry of noise and movement. Down the length of the street twenty, maybe thirty, dogs rushed wildly ahead, some crashing blindly into the barricades, only to ricochet into the street and continue their headlong flight. Victor wondered how the beasts were able to run at all: they were little more than patchworks of fur and scarred flesh slapped helter-skelter on bony skeletons. Right behind the ragged pack of dogs came the motorcycles—four deep and in perfect formation. Atop each bike was a policeman in full uniform, each waving a long wooden club and howling wildly at his quarry.

With the sighting of the first dog the random noise of the crowd had changed to a steady, repetitive plea: "Kill! Kill! Kill!" Almost directly in front of Victor, the spectators got their wish. A small mongrel, lagging behind the pack with a broken leg, took a vicious spill, its momentum rolling it over and over, crushing the already shattered limb against the pavement again and again. The animal finally came to rest on a manhole cover in the center of the street, whimpering softly, unable to get up. For a moment the dog was all alone, some grotesque still-life form caught between two walls of motion. In that instant Victor could see it clearly, could see its eyes more quizzical than terrorized, almost as if, in that final second, it had learned to wonder why. And then the motorcycles were upon it, and as the crowd cheered them on the two policemen in the center of each line clubbed the dog to a pulp as they passed by.

All around Victor the crowd was surging past, moving down the line of barricades in pursuit of the motorcycles. Everyone but Marba. He remained propped up against the barrier, watching the battered corpse in the street. There was no expression on his face.

"What now?" Victor gestured in the direction in which everyone was heading.

Marba didn't vary his gaze. "Go with them or you'll miss the end of it. Pick me up when you get back."

"You sure?"

"Yeah, when you get back."

"All right then . . . you'll be okay?"

Marba didn't answer.

"Okay," Victor repeated, and set out after the crowd.

It was obvious that the spectators knew where they were going. By taking a shortcut across Ninety-fourth Street, they reached the park in advance of the dogs and motorcycles, which had traveled up and down Amsterdam and Columbus avenues for several blocks before turning up Central Park West. By the time Victor caught up with the crowd almost all the sight lines were taken. People stood fifteen and twenty deep on a grassy knoll overlooking a large wooden pen, their numbers swelled by others who had joined them along the route, and it was only by scrambling atop an already crowded tour bus that he was afforded a view.

Next to Victor two ladies were talking enthusiastically, checking out their movie cameras for the action just moments away. Both wore bright red buttons with the words CITY SAFARI in green letters around the edges. "They won't believe this in Akron," Victor heard one of the ladies titter as she focused her camera on the enclosure.

"No roundup was ever like this," agreed her companion, dropping her camera to her side. "I'm too nervous to take pictures—you get 'em for us."

"I will and . . . I see them!"

Into the park they came. More dogs this time, followed by the sixteen cyclists in close pursuit. Victor was amazed that the animals were still on their feet—was it rage or fear that drove them those final yards into the pen? As soon as the dogs and motorcycles had passed into the wooden enclosure, a wire screen was rolled across the entrance, making escape impossible.

Then the carnage began. While the dogs scrambled frantically from one side of the pen to the other, the policemen rode methodically among them, flailing away at the beasts with their clubs. Every time a dog fell, the crowd erupted in a cheer. Near the end, the ground got so slippery with blood that the motorcycles would skid and roll over. When this happened the policemen would leap from their mounts and set out on foot, crushing the skulls of the dogs as they cowered against the walls or ran helplessly in senseless circles.

It was over quickly. Suddenly the last dog was crumbling to the ground and the tour guide was urging his passengers to please board the bus. The carnival spirit that held the crowd together evaporated and the people dispersed hastily in all directions, casting wary glances at other individuals who walked nearby. In less than ten minutes the park was deserted.

Marba was still leaning against the barricade when Victor returned. Out in the street, oblivious to Marba's presence, an old man in a long, tattered overcoat was bending over the lifeless form of the small dog with the quizzical eyes. He stooped there for several minutes, as if he was trying to make up his mind about something. Then he reached under his coat and pulled out a faded shopping bag. Picking up the dog corpse by the tail, he lowered it carefully into the bag. All the while Marba was watching intently, his eyes shifting ever so slightly to follow the old man's every move.

Victor didn't approach the lieutenant until the old man had tucked the sack back under his coat and shuffled off out of sight. "Look," he said, seeing that Marba was disturbed and trying to make him feel better, "at least the dog will get a decent burial."

Marba turned to face Victor squarely. "What makes you think that?"

"You saw the old man take him away—it was probably his dog."

"You *don't* know New York," Marba said sadly, shaking his head and walking slowly toward the car. "The only burial that dog will get is in a garbage can—after it's been eaten."

The ride down to Oasis Two began in silence; Marba hunched sullenly at the wheel of the car, his face waxy and strained; Victor sitting next to him, thinking of ways to bring him out of his stupor. There were urgent questions to be asked of Marba—his behavior at the dogging had convinced Victor of that. Could a man displaying such emotional paralysis function effectively on the case? Victor suspected not, but he needed more than suspicions if he was to reopen the issue of Marba's command competence with Central Operations.

"Are those doggings held very often?" Victor asked, trying to generate some conversation.

Marba stared out the windshield, saying nothing.

"Are they on a regular basis?" he prodded, this time with more success.

Marba spoke, his lips moving ever so slightly against the tightness of his face. "Sorry . . . you saw me like that out there. . . ."

"Don't worry about it," Victor replied after a few moments, surprised by Marba's admission.

"No, really. I am sorry. It's just that sometimes . . . seeing that . . . I mean—it's one thing to get rid of the dog packs . . . I'm as much against rabies and mauled kids as the next guy . . . but to make a tourist attraction of it and advertise it in the travel brochures—"

"I understand," Victor interrupted. "I just don't see why you took me up there in the first place if it disturbs you so much."

"I wanted you to see it so you'd know what's happening to New York and why some of us want to do something about changing it."

Victor measured Marba carefully with his eyes. "It's changed you. At the academy they still call you Old

Rockhard. And I must say," Victor admitted, "for a while last night I thought they were right."

Marba stiffened. "They were . . . and they still are. You people will never understand that a sense of compassion is not a sign of weakness. What the hell are they teaching you down there anyway? How to rip the heart right out of your body?" Marba glared at his passenger. "You want to see Old Rockhard?" he shouted, upcharging the car and hurtling it forward for emphasis. "For your sake, you better hope you never do."

Victor gritted his teeth. He could detect the tingle starting in the palm of his hand, sense the exquisite desire to ram it full force into Marba's face, almost feel the bone and cartilage as it buckled under the blow and splintered into the old man's brain. Marba personified everything he had been taught to detest: a man with a broken body and a crippled mind; a man whose behavior was not a product of logic and expedience but, rather, whim and sentimentality. That made Marba's behavior a mystery—and Victor could ill afford to work with mysteries. Nor would he—and this time he'd make sure of it.

Up ahead the World Trade towers loomed into view, giant metal fingers protruding from the cupped parapets that sealed them into Oasis Two. Marba drove relentlessly toward them, like an arrow thrust to the target by some unseen fury. The fragment of conversation that had plunged the two men into conflict was never finished, and the ride to the Oasis ended as it had begun—in silence.

The command briefing room in Oasis Two had been a private conference room for Wall Street insiders until most of them fled the city and the police department took up temporary residence there. It was a richly appointed chamber, replete with teakwood floors, mahogany longtables, and a huge marble podium; and as Victor shouldered his way into the crowded enclosure he was struck by the incongruity of New York cops using the place as an assembly area.

Up front at the marble rostrum a man had just begun speaking. "Officers . . . please . . ." he was saying, "time is precious—let's not waste it!" Victor recognized him immediately as Captain Anderson, the director of Oasis Security who had spoken to him over the videophone. "I want to turn this briefing over to Commissioner Charles," he continued, speaking steadily until the din around him had died away and his voice was the only sound audible. "He has the latest update on the case. Once he's finished, you'll all receive your assignments." Anderson turned from the podium, moved quickly across the elevated marble walkway, and down to his front row seat. Then, almost as if on cue, a paneled door swung open and a second man approached the rostrum. Every person in the room rose and began clapping rhythmically, their hands moving in unison above their heads. The commissioner acknowledged their greeting and then waved for silence.

"As you all know, yesterday at 3:20 P.M., Ms. Helen Stenley, Federal Commissioner of Housing, was kidnapped on the outskirts of Oasis One as she prepared to embark on a tour of the Displaced People's Zones." The commissioner paused and looked around the room. "The gravity of this event cannot be underestimated by anyone here," he cautioned grimly. "The fact that this is the first major crime in an Oasis this year is bad enough. We work like dogs to convince the public they can come here with minds at ease, and then one sensational crime spoils the whole effort. But the damage to our reputation as a safe city is not the most serious result of this crime."

Leaning forward, the commissioner curled his hands around the podium and tapped the marble with his fingers as he spoke. "The problem with this particular crime is that it lends credibility to Stenley's charges—no matter how ridiculous, no matter how unsubstantiated, no matter how biased they are. And," he warned, his voice rising slightly, "every hour that woman remains missing, she gains more publicity, more public sympathy. At the same time we gain a greater black eye," he added. "Just before I arrived here I heard that some morning papers are already suggesting we might benefit greatly if Stenley doesn't turn up, or turns up dead."

An undercurrent of angry voices spread throughout the room.

"I assure you, I share your feelings," the commissioner granted, "and that is why it is necessary that we crack this case and get the Stenley woman back alive . . . fast."

"We'll do it," a voice from the middle of the room exclaimed.

"Yes . . . yes . . ." others in the audience agreed optimistically.

"Wait a moment . . . it won't be that easy. For one, I know some of you don't exactly like the Stenley woman."

A hearty chorus of laughter greeted the commissioner's observation.

"And we have very little to go on." The commissioner activated the projection cubicle from the control panel on the rostrum. "Look at this. . . ."

Directly behind the speaker's platform a large, trisurface screen dropped into place.

"Here is a comp-ed version of the kidnapping." The briefing room lights dimmed automatically and the edited film began to run. "Because the kidnapping occurred after the victim left her press conference, there weren't any professional photographers around. Thus, we didn't get any holographic or Kirlean images—and what we did get was shot by amateurs and not very helpful. . . . Here comes the relevant footage."

The wavy lines on the screen resolved themselves into the Stenley woman sitting between two Oasis guards in the back seat of a slowly moving police cruiser. "This was shot at Fifty-eighth and Sixth, on the way to the Central Park checkpoint. Now watch this," the commissioner alerted, pointing to the upper left edge of the screen, where a man, his back to the camera, was stepping into the street waving a petition in the air. "I'll halt here," he said, pushing the stop-action control button, "so you can get a look at our suspect. It's the only shot we have of him or anyone else we believe is connected with the crime."

Victor stared intently at the profile of the man frozen on the screen, trying to detect some telltale characteristic. He found none.

"Now here's the last actual footage you'll see before the cruiser moves out of camera range." The commissioner released the stop-action button and the still form sprang to life, jogging up to the police vehicle and tapping at the steelglas plating with the end of the tightly rolled petition. Inside the cruiser, the Stenley woman was motioning the driver to stop. After an animated exchange of words between the two he did stop, lowering the cruiser's forward shielding so that his front gunner could reach out and take the petition from the unidentified man. Then he drove on, out of viewing range. The screen went wavy again.

"That was a terrible mistake," the commissioner interjected, halting the film. "We didn't expect any trouble— but the officers were instructed to keep the shields raised at all times just in case. And to accept that petition from a total stranger . . ." he grimaced, "it just defies explanation. . . ."

"Excuse me, sir."

The commissioner peered around the partially darkened room to locate the voice that had interrupted him.

"Here . . ." it was Steve Mott, a reporter for the Long Island *Times*, a man highly partial to NYPD affairs and one of the three newsmen allowed to attend departmental briefings.

"What is it?" Charles asked, recognizing the reporter.

"I'm not trying to excuse the officers for what they did, but hadn't the Stenley woman received several such petitions from unidentified citizens throughout the day?"

"Yes . . . but all under tight police surveillance . . . and all of them were examined before she was allowed to keep any."

"But the man in the film handed the petition to the gunner, not Stenley—don't you think he checked it out before he gave it to her?"

"Probably so," the commissioner observed, "but as you'll see, the perpetrator obviously figured on that."

Mott shook his head, a puzzled expression on his face.

"Let me illustrate. . . ." The commissioner fingered the projection cubicle and a new image flashed into view. "From here on the film you'll be seeing is computer simulated—based on the combined reports of witnesses and evidence found at the scene. It suggests pictorially our best hunch as to what actually transpired between Fifty-eighth Street and the kidnapping on Central Park Mall."

On the screen an animated facsimile of the police cruiser continued down Sixth Avenue, through the checkpoint, and into Central Park on schedule. It moved without incident past the pond and the zoo on its way to Seventy-second Street. Then, without warning, it swerved back and forth like a novice sailor with no sea legs, coming to rest against a traffic barrier separating the road from the mall. Almost simultaneously a helicopter dropped into view, landing a few feet from the immobilized vehicle and disgorging three hooded men carrying thermal-laser cutters. The men moved directly to the cruiser and cut through the rear shielding in precise, carefully calibrated movements. As the steelglas fell away a substance like escaping steam drifted into the air. Two of the men lifted the limp body of the Stenley woman from the back seat and carried her toward the aircraft, while the third member of the team remained temporarily behind to behead the Oasis guards with three short bursts of the thermal-laser. Once this was done, he too returned to the helicopter, which took off and headed in a northeasterly direction.

The briefing room lights came back on as the triscreen went blank. "The whole helicopter operation—from touchdown to liftoff—took about ninety seconds, according to our best estimates," the commissioner noted, a hint of admiration in his voice. "There were no prints, no respiration or salivary residues, not even any configurational byprods . . . it was a clean job—it's as simple as that. We did find this, however." Charles gestured to Captain Anderson, who held up a five-foot photo enlargement of a ruptured, slightly charred object. "The petition," he explained. "It was found in the gunner's compartment. Which gets us back to Mr. Mott's questions. It is our theory that the man you saw in the film gave the petition to the gunner knowing full well that it would be examined. But he also knew that before the examination could be completed the petition would detonate, dispersing concussion gas through the cruiser. He knew this because the gas was placed inside the wooden pin attached to the end of the petition—in a place where the entire scroll would have to be unwound before it could be inspected." The commissioner rubbed at the back of his neck vigorously. "A well-wrapped Trojan horse—that's what the petition was. It was a beautiful plan: they hit us inside the Oasis when our guards were down—and then they finished us off outside the Oasis, when our guards were helpless."

For a moment the commissioner stopped talking and just stared out into space. When he did speak again it was slow and deliberate, through clenched teeth. "Those men made fools of us—fools of every man on this force. I want those men. I want every one of them—and I want them *now*, this morning, this minute." Then, with his hands coiled into fists, he turned abruptly from the podium and strode quickly out of the room—leaving Captain Anderson with the somewhat awesome task of coordinating the largest manhunt in New York history.

CHAPTER FOUR

Across from the skating rink at Rockefeller Center the tour buses were lined up and ready to go. With their heavy steel-gray frames and flared rear plating they resembled armored whales waiting to plunge into the Hudson River. Directly in front of the first bus a pitchman, complete with cane and megaphone, was hawking the tour to everyone within earshot. "Do you want to ride the prime time crime line?" he would shout enthusiastically. And there were plenty of takers who did. About every fifteen minutes the front bus would fill up—at twenty dollars a head—and roll out on a two-hour tour of, as the barker put it, "the outer city."

Victor watched for Marty from the edge of the crowd that had gathered to hear the pitchman sell his wares. Two hours had elapsed since the Oasis Two briefing and he was impatient to get on with his plans. "Damn these updates," he muttered, turning his attention to the barker as a means of keeping his mind off his work.

The pitchman was a virtuoso. "Gather 'round," he said, beckoning with his cane. "I'm gonna tell you a story—true story 'bout darkest Affreeca. Seems one New Yorker was planning to hunt right there on the Dark Continent. His friend got worried and said, 'You take care . . . I've heard it's dangerous there.' And you know what that travelwise New Yorker replied?" The barker made a flourish with his cane. "He said, 'I feel safer in the jungle than the streets of New York—at least I'm the hunter and I've got the gun.'"

The crowd laughed.

"Oh, that's not funneee, ladies and gentlemen—that hunter, he was right, you know. He was *dead* right. I mean, what do they have over in that Affreeca anyway? A few tigers—a lion or two—hell, with those new game preserves you can't shoot them and they're so well fed they don't have room to eat you."

More laughter.

"Ahhh, but New York . . . now, that's different. You can get shot here—yessireee—knifed, too, just like in Tarzan's day. Now don't get me wrong, you fine folks out there. I don't want to scare you away—nosireee—and I don't want to get you hurt, either. And you know why?" The pitchman flipped his cane into the air like a baton and caught it with the point toward the spectators. "Because I love you. And because I love you I'll tell you what I'm gonna do. I'm gonna offer you a chance of a lifetime—a chance to enjoy all the excitement and mystery of the most dangerous jungle of all—the jungle of Manhattan— from the comfort and safety of our air-conditioned, armor-plated safari coach. And, ladies and gentlemen," the barker lowered his voice, "I want you to know that if things get a little too exciting out there . . . well, there's a bathroom aboard."

The crowd could hardly restrain itself.

"Now listen, you nice folks . . ." the pitchman coaxed through his megaphone, waiting for the noise to subside, "in a moment I'm going to let you step right up—plunk down the small twenty-dollar fare—that's right, only twenty dollars—and get yourself ready for the most memorable trip of a lifetime. But before I do, you might be asking yourself: 'What'll I see for my money?'" The barker danced about gleefully. "Well, you gentle people —I'm glad you asked that question. Of course, there's no way to guarantee what will happen on any particular trip—that's part of the excitement. But I can tell you this: less than a week ago bus number 46 left from this very spot—and before it returned two hours later the lucky passengers inside had witnessed first hand—in person now —no Hollywood make-believe—not one, but *two* crimes. That's right, I said *two* criminal offenses: an armed robbery, and that most heinous of acts, the assault of a young woman." The barker was waving his cane around like a mad swordsman, as if he were trying to skewer every word that tumbled out of his mouth. "And if that's not enough," he thrusted, "on their way back to the Oasis, these same passengers observed the body of a young boy —dead, I'm sorry to say, of a drug overdose."

Suddenly the cane waving stopped and the pitchman stepped closer to the line of bystanders. "Now I ask you seriously—each one of you—where are you going to get thrills like that for your money? On television? Holographics? The backyard barbecue? No, sir, ladieees and gentlemen—if you want that kind of action, you're gonna hafta ride with us—right now—on the prime time crime line. So step right up—the big safari coach will be leaving in just a few minutes. . . ."

With a final flourish of his cane the barker waved the spectators forward and then braced himself as a goodly portion of the crowd surged around him, twenty-dollar bills at the ready.

Victor watched the pitchman go through his act twice before Marty arrived and bought her ticket. She timed the purchase perfectly, waiting until an empty bus rolled up to the loading platform before she put down her twenty dollars. When Victor bought his ticket and boarded the bus a few minutes later, it was only half full and he had no difficulty getting a seat next to her. "Hello," he said cordially as he swung into the outside seat. She acknowledged his greeting and then turned back to the window. It would be the last thing either of them would say to each other until the tour was well underway.

At the front of the bus a man wearing army fatigues and a gun was talking through a microphone, discussing equipment and security procedures aboard the vehicle as it pulled cumbersomely away from the curb. It reminded Victor of the canned address the airline stewardesses presented just before takeoff. The contents of the message and the perfunctory way in which it was delivered didn't seem to dampen the enthusiasm of the passengers, however. They talked in nervous, excited little gasps, gripping their cameras and each other—craning their necks to peer out the window so as not to miss a moment of any violence that might be lurking in the vicinity. By the time the bus had moved out beyond the final Oasis checkpoint, things were at such a fever pitch that the slightest mention of crime was enough to send shockwaves of anticipation surging through the passengers.

Next to Victor, Marty was listening to the tour guide describe how newsreels of famous crimes would be flashed on a screen behind the driver as the bus passed by the places where they had been committed. Victor caught a glimpse of her as he leaned forward to adjust his seat. She was the best regional supervisor in the country—of that he had no doubt. But then, he had had very little doubt about anything since he'd joined Psycor.

Victor leaned back and let his mind wander—back to the memory of another bus ride—back to when he was very young. Strange, he thought, how little that time

meant anymore, how meaningless his early life had become. Just bits and snatches of recollections—that was all.
Like the recollection of the big orange bus carrying him
home from second grade. How it had stopped in front of
his house and how surprised he'd been when he stepped
off and saw all the grownups standing around. He had
tried to get inside but one of the neighbor women had
lifted him off his feet and asked if he wanted to play with
her for a while. And right then he knew something bad
had happened and that his mother was dead.

A sharp bump jolted Victor out of his reverie. Up front,
the driver had maneuvered the left half of his bus onto
the curb and come to a stop, half in the street and half
on the sidewalk. At the same time the armed guide was
pointing to a shattered storefront on the corner of Eighty-
third and Lexington. "Take a close look on your right, if
you would, please," he said, "and you will see the spot
where three armed bandits died trying to hold up a liquor
store. This particular shootout has quite an interesting
story behind it—a story that became nationally known
when it was immortalized in the popular song 'A Shop-
keeper's Revenge.'"

"I remember that one," a chubby youngster volunteered
from the front of the bus:

"Old Mr. Willis had been robbed six times before
but on the fateful seventh he evened up the score. . . ."

"That's right, son," the guide replied encouragingly.
"Do you remember the whole song?"

"I think so. . . ."

"Well then, why don't you come right up here with me
and tell the people what happened while I show them
some slides of the robbery?"

The boy hesitated, but his mother shoved him, gently but firmly, out of his seat and into the aisle. "All right . . ." he agreed, and shuffled his way over to the guide.

"Now you hold on to this," the guide instructed, handing the boy his microphone, "and I'll tell you when to start talking. First, though, I want everyone to see how this area looked both before and after the shootout occurred." The guide fingered a small control panel on the armrest of his seat and waited while darkout filters automatically slid into place over the passenger windows; then he flipped a lever and two pictures flashed on the miniature viewing screen behind the driver's seat.

"You'll note here the building on the corner," the guide said, walking over to the screen and using a pointer to identify a structure on the leftmost slide. "That is the liquor store before the robbery attempt. Note that although the buildings around it are in various stages of decay, the store itself is in relatively good shape. Also pay special attention to these cars on the street—the ones with the arrows above them. Here . . . and here . . ." he instructed, tapping the screen where the small red arrows were situated. "Now compare the 'before' photo with the 'after' photo next to it—taken just moments after the holdup attempt."

The second picture looked like a study at ground zero. The front of the liquor store was nothing more than a gaping hole—blown to bits as if a bomb had exploded behind it. Shattered glass and fragments of twisted metal were strewn over the street—along with three bodies and a good deal of blood. The two cars which had been parked in front of the store—the ones designated with red arrows—had also been mangled: their tires flattened, windows smashed, and bodies riddled with holes.

The guide turned to his control panel for a moment and

announced, "I'll leave both pictures on the screen and you can compare them with what you see outside again." As he spoke the darkout filters lifted, once again providing the passengers with an unobstructed view of the street. "It'll be more difficult to see the slides in this light," he admitted, "but you'll be able to see enough to make the important comparisons. What I believe you'll find most amazing is how unchanged the street looks right now from the way it appears in the photo taken right after the attempted robbery. Yet that photo is almost three years old. We have our historically minded sanitation department to thank for this landmark preservation—they've been kind enough to leave the destruction and debris almost untouched since that fateful day."

Victor noted that only a few of the passengers realized that the guide was joking. The rest of them would probably return to their home towns thinking that the New York Sanitation Department was a public-spirited, civic-minded organization.

"Now then, young man," the guide exclaimed, smiling at the youngster holding the microphone, "we've kept you waiting a little while, haven't we?"

The boy giggled nervously and fidgeted with a button on his shirt.

"What's your name?"

"Timmy," the boy replied, still giggling.

"Well, Timmy, how old are you?"

"Eleven."

"That's nice. Listen, Timmy, while your parents and their friends are looking over the famous crime site, why don't you tell us what happened? That's right," he coaxed, "talk right into the microphone."

"There was this guy—Mr. Willis. . . ."

"Go on."

"He owned the liquor store. Guys had been holding him up, though—and he was scared."

"How many times had he been stuck up?"

"Six."

"And had anybody been caught?"

Timmy shook his head.

"So what did he decide to do about it?"

"He bought some guns."

"Do you remember what kinds?"

"Yes . . . it's in the song. A shotgun, a magnum, and a .44."

"Do you know anything about those guns, young man?"

"Nope."

"They're very powerful."

"Oh," said Timmy, twisting the microphone cord around his hand.

"So then what happened?"

"Three guys came in and tried to stick up the store. Mr. Willis gave them the money and when they were going out the door, he reached under the counter and pulled out a gun."

"And . . . ?"

"He told them to stop or he'd shoot."

"Did they?"

"No . . . so he shot at them."

"Did they stop when he fired his first shot?"

"I don't think so."

"Why not?"

"It says in the song that he used three guns."

"Oh? Do you remember how that part of the song went?"

"Yep."

"Will you sing it for us?"

"I can't sing," Timmy admitted, giggling again.

"Just say the words, then."

Timmy looked down the aisle at his mother.

"Go ahead and say them," the guide urged.

"First he tried his magnum, and then his .44;
He even used his shotgun, and the robbers were no more.
So pity those poor hoodlums who tried to rob his store;
Mr. Willis fed them lead, and blew them out the door."

"That's quite a song, isn't it, Timmy?"

"Yes, sir."

"So he fired all those guns to stop the robbers. Do you know why?"

Timmy thought for a moment. "I don't."

"No trouble, son. I'll tell everyone why." The guide patted Timmy on the back. "What they don't say in the song—and what Timmy didn't know—is that Mr. Willis had never fired a gun before he began blasting away during the holdup."

Statements of disbelief echoed through the bus.

"I know it's hard to believe, but it's true," the guide assured his doubtful listeners. "It seems that our Mr. Willis got so disgusted after being held up six times that he went to a friend who knew firearms and asked what type of gun he should buy to best defend himself. The friend recommended the shotgun, .357 magnum, and the .44 caliber revolver as good bets because they all were powerful enough to stop an assailant with one shot." The tour guide broke out in a wide grin. "What the friend didn't realize is that Willis went out and purchased all three guns—hid them, loaded, near the cash register—and waited for any would-be robbers to appear. When—"

"Can I ask a question?" A middle-aged man near the back of the bus broke in.

"Sure."

"Those guns you mentioned—they have tremendous kicks. How could he have been accurate enough to hit those robbers without any training?"

"The way he fired those guns he didn't need much accuracy! And that's the most incredible part of the story. When the thieves failed to heed his warning on their way out of the store, Willis simply picked up the magnum in both hands, closed his eyes, and emptied it. Then he repeated the performance with the .44 and the shotgun —firing blindly until the ammunition ran out."

"What about the robbers?" asked the wife of the middle-aged man. "Did they just stand there and let him keep shooting like that?"

"Lady," the tour guide observed, shaking his head, "when somebody starts firing a cannon in your direction you either hit the floor or run like hell. In the case of the three dead robbers, it looks like they hit the floor. And as you can see from the slide or by looking out the window—there was no floor left when Willis stopped shooting."

"But wasn't he arrested for all that?" the woman wanted to know.

"On what charge? Self-defense? No," the guide replied, "not only were no charges filed against him, but he became a kind of instant hero to crime-weary New Yorkers. The miracle was that no innocent bystanders got injured in the gunfire."

The lady turned to her husband. "It's worse than those barbarians in the Westerns," she said in a voice loud enough so everyone could hear.

"Well, take a good last look," the guide suggested, getting up and walking Timmy back to his seat, "because you ain't seen nothin' yet. If you check your tour map

you'll see that our next stop will take us right into the
heart of Morningside Heights—an area with one of the
highest crime rates in the city—and give us a chance to
see the place where the Unknown Sniper mowed down
ten innocent people last year." The guide signaled the bus
driver to pull out. "Meanwhile, I'd like to point out some
other scenes of interest along the way. For example, the
burned-out building that will be coming up on your left,
at the corner of Park Avenue . . ."

Victor listened to the guide awhile longer, then turned
his head toward the window and in a soft but audible
voice asked, "Some trip, eh?"

"I've heard this guy before," Marty answered, reflexively scanning the area around her to make sure
nobody was listening to their conversation. "Wait till he
gets to Chelsea, where some kids were ripped apart by a
dog pack a while back."

Victor frowned. "This city has gone to hell—I think I'll
exercise my assignment option on the West Coast from
now on."

Marty took a cigarette out of her bag and lit up. "You're
not happy with this assignment?"

"It's not that exactly . . . I asked for it in the first place.
But not—"

"As Marba's assistant . . . ?"

"You know?"

"Yes. Why do you think I moved this meeting up a
day?"

"I don't follow. . . ."

"You don't follow Marba very well, either." Marty took
a deep drag on her cigarette and let the smoke escape
slowly between her lips. "He called me this morning during a break in the briefing. Seems you haven't made a hit
with our lieutenant."

"That son of a bitch," Victor said flatly.

"I didn't know Psycor agents made a habit of denegrating their command officers."

"He's no command officer," Victor scoffed, "and you know it."

"Central Operations wouldn't agree."

"They will soon enough," Victor replied confidently, rubbing the knuckles on his right hand. "I was going to submit an appeal on his appointment tonight. Now that you're here, I'll save the time and initiate proceedings through your office immediately."

"Don't waste the effort."

"I tell you, the man is dangerous. He's not capable of leadership: I saw that today at a dogging. He fell apart, mentally and physically he disintegrated. He could endanger the whole mission."

"Don't waste the effort," she repeated.

Victor leaned over and took hold of Marty's arm. "You don't understand. The man is senile—a human wasteland."

Marty twisted away from Victor's grip. "No, *you* don't understand. You think Central Operations doesn't know about Marba? You think we're all so stupid and you're the only one with eyes?" Marty jammed her cigarette into the ashtray in front of her. "You younger agents are really something," she said, shaking her head. "Now let me tell you something: the reason why Marba is in command of this assignment—and the reason he will be *staying* in command—is because he has contacts and information we need to solve the kidnapping."

"Information, eh?"

"Yes, information and people. Didn't Marba make plans to meet with you later this afternoon?"

"So what?"

"And didn't he say something about bringing over some important materials?"

"Sure," Victor admitted, "he *said* that. But after what else he said this morning, what reason is there to believe him?"

"Why don't you look at the materials before you make up your mind?"

"It's crazy." Victor slumped back in his seat. "The man is a disgrace to Psycor."

"Like I said," Marty repeated, "let the evidence speak for itself. We all know Marba's a problem, but you have the skills to cope with him . . . if you're willing to try."

"Enter the flattery approach," Victor said sarcastically.

"I'm familiar with your record, Mr. Slaughter," Marty replied dryly. "I'm sure you don't need to be told how good you are. But remember this—while you're in this state I still outrank you. And I'm saying that Marba remains in command."

"And Central Operations . . . ?"

"That's what they say, too."

Victor shrugged. "I guess that's that."

"I believe so," Marty concurred, turning back to the window. They were the final words she spoke on the tour.

Across the aisle from Victor, two teen-age girls had spread a tour map over their laps and were studiously following the course of the trip, listening for the guide's description of their location and then gesturing excitedly when they spotted the point along the route.

"We're coming into an area now," the guide announced, "which is one of the most rundown in the city."

"Here . . . see . . ." one of the girls whispered, tapping the map with her finger, "the Bowery."

"Judging from the dilapidated buildings and rubble in

the streets, you might think that this area is uninhabited. If you do, you're wrong. People do live here, people with no place else to go. Years back that meant primarily winos and bums, but lately they've been joined by other 'down and outers'—the elderly, the infirm, the desperately poor."

A teen-ager in the seat behind the driver piped up, "I know them, they're Dregs."

"That's enough, Bill," the boy's father warned.

"The young man is right. That's what they're called here in New York. And if you consider their way of life you'll begin to understand—"

The guide was cut off in midsentence by the sharp blast of a siren. CRIME ALERT! Somewhere, somebody had pressed the small red button over their seat and turned the bus into an explosion of color and sound. From the back of every seat, hidden speakers emitted a warbling signal, while above them a message panel spelled out CRIME REPORTED—STAND BY in flashing blue lights. At the same time, beams of light shot out from the ceiling of the bus, reflecting off the windows and bathing everything in an eerie red glow. And above it all, over and over, a mechanical voice kept repeating: "Don't panic—this is a crime alert—stand by for further instructions. . . . Don't panic—this is a crime alert—stand by for further instructions. . . ."

If there was anything resembling panic aboard the bus, it was the shoving and pushing of the passengers as they scrambled to get a better view of the suspected crime, which was in progress a half block away. Even the girls across from Victor had forsaken their map for a look outside, their bodies twisted toward the window like sunflowers seeking light, their faces jammed flush against the steelglas so as not to miss a thing.

As the bus pulled forward for a better view, it did seem

that a crime was underway: five tattered old men were lurching about the gutter on their hands and knees, bumping and butting each other, their stubbled, drawn faces pinched into hideous expressions of rage. Yet the careful observer could tell that things weren't as they appeared to be. For one, the driver made no attempt to call in a CIP (crime in progress); also, the guide had an expression of boredom on his face. Victor glanced over at Marty to see if she knew what was taking place. She was also straining to see out the window—and he couldn't be sure if she was doing it for real or for show.

The guide waited silently until the bus had passed slowly by the scene of the melee, turned, and driven by a second time—affording passengers on both sides a clear view of the proceedings. Then he announced, a hint of disappointment in his voice, "What you are witnessing is not a crime—just a bit of teen-age horseplay."

Several of the tourists looked at each other blankly.

"You people on the left, do you see that Mazda parked about a hundred feet back of us?"

There was a chorus of yeses.

"Can you tell if anybody is in there from this distance?"

"Looks like four, maybe five guys," a man in front of Victor spoke up.

"Can you estimate how old they are?"

"Eighteen . . . maybe nineteen . . . somewhere around there."

"That sounds about right. What those kids do is cruise around this neighborhood looking for drunks who live on the benches you see lining the park side of the street. When they spot five or six who are sober enough to be sitting up, they drive by slowly, roll down their window, and throw out handfuls of nickels into the gutter. Then they park nearby and watch the bums scramble into the street and fight with each other over the money."

The guide's explanation of what was happening didn't seem to disturb many of the tourists. Most of them continued to gawk at two remaining derelicts still crawling around the gutter looking for nickels.

"Let's move out," the guide told his driver, satisfied that everyone had seen enough. He wasn't totally correct. The bus was barely underway when a second group of derelicts was spotted sitting on three rickety benches near the curb.

"Can we stop for a second?" It was the man in front of Victor speaking again.

"What for?" the guide wanted to know.

"I'd like to get a shot of them going for the money," he answered, gesturing toward the old men.

The guide thought for a moment. "I don't see why not— we've got a few minutes."

The driver pulled over directly across the street from the benches.

"Do you have any nickels?" the guide asked.

"Better than that," the man responded gleefully, "this is going to be a real scramble." He turned to his wife. "Honey, give me that roll of quarters I brought for tolls . . . and hand me my camera, too, will ya?"

Outside, the men on the benches began observing the bus with growing interest. "They've been this route before," Victor muttered under his breath, watching as two or three of them weaved forward on the edge of their seats.

Inside, the man whose suggestion had brought the bus to a halt was moving to the front, forty quarters clenched in his fist. "Can I shoot from outside?" he asked the guide, gesturing with his head toward the camera slung over his left shoulder.

"Sorry, not allowed. Why don't you shoot from behind this steelglas panel after you throw out the money?" he suggested.

"Okay. Can I throw it now?"

"Anytime you're ready," the guide responded, sliding back the panel.

As soon as the panel opened, the occupants of the benches began gesturing frantically, pointing and shouting at the small venthole. It was quite a scene. The man with the handful of quarters, his arm cocked, poised like some politico about to throw out the first ball of the season; the decaying old men, their bodies braced against the benches, hunched over like macabre sprinters ready to burst from their starting blocks; the tourists, filling the windows with Nikons and Polaroids, resembling an aggregate of news photographers gone amok.

Then the man's hand was traveling forward and the quarters were tumbling into the street, spinning and rolling against the curb and onto the sidewalk. For an instant the old men froze, stunned by the sight of quarters rather than pennies or nickels, then there was a frenzy of movement as they stumbled and staggered after the money. A cheer went up from the bus as the men broke for the street, followed by individual shouts of encouragement as the tourists picked out their favorite derelicts and cheered them on. Not that the old men needed any urging: five quarters would buy a cheap bottle of wine, and that sent them into the fray with a sense of divine purpose.

The action was furious and short-lived. There were two or three minutes of cursing and shoving, with the men scuttling along the gutter like wounded crabs, and then it was all over. Miraculously, all the combatants were able to drag themselves back to their benches, where (by what must have been some prearranged agreement) each was allowed to count his share of the booty in peace.

As it turned out, the derelicts provided the most exciting moments on the tour. The rest of the trip was movies and slides, crime scenes and stories of lawless mayhem. Yet the passengers never lost their sense of anticipation. Like novice fishermen on their first deep-sea excursion, each person waited for that ripple of activity signaling the action he craved. When it didn't come, and the bus returned safely and promptly to the Oasis, there was a natural letdown. Still, the tourists seemed generally satisfied with their experience. "After all," the man sitting in front of Victor summed it up to his wife, "you can't expect to win the lottery every time you buy a ticket. Besides," he observed, "we *did* have fun. Watching those bums, I mean—it sure beat feeding pigeons!"

CHAPTER FIVE

Victor Slaughter didn't look the part of a man doing top-level, dangerous law-enforcement work. Sitting on the corner of his bed, watching TV and waiting for Marba to arrive, he rather resembled a clerk or salesman. Which suited Psycor fine. The last thing they wanted was conspicuous operatives.

Victor was about as inconspicuous as a person could be. He looked so normal, in fact, one might think he was designed from a statistical profile of the "average" American. Even his face was nondescript: the features common, the contours standard. If a criminal had been blessed with such an appearance, one could only pity his victims—there was little chance they could ever pick him out of a lineup or identify him in a mugbook. There was no noticeable characteristic to grab hold of, no special idiosyncrasy to help jog the memory. Victor was often amused by the antics of his more distinctive-looking colleagues who used disguises to keep their cover. It was nice to know that one's own appearance was the best disguise of all—yet Victor hadn't come by his camouflage easily. First there had been the endless hours of postural conditioning and the tedium of facial-control exercises. Then there was the plastic surgery. Victor hadn't liked that at all. Submitting to muscular reshape was one thing—but to surgically alter one's appearance, that was another matter. Only after a good deal of procrastination had he finally consented to the operations, and then in a less than enthusiastic manner. Finally, there was the need to adjust to a new physical appearance. Getting accustomed to a new face hadn't been easy for Victor; next to personality realignment, it was the most difficult adjustment he'd had to make during Psycor training.

Sometimes Victor would study himself in a mirror and try to gauge how much he had changed. There had been a significant transformation, of that there was no doubt; yet it was when he peered beneath the facial sheath into his own mind that the greatest metamorphosis was revealed. Before personality realignment, Victor wouldn't have believed such a transformation possible; but then, he couldn't have been expected to know how far Psycor had developed the tools and knowledge of behavioral science. Nor could he have realized that his genetic endowment and personality characteristics made him uniquely suited to become a Psycor operative. Psycor realized it, though, and they capitalized on their knowledge from the first day he reached their training base.

Of all the days he'd spent during four years of intensive Psycor training, Victor remembered that first day best of all. Particularly the incident at IPCEN. He had been ushered into a room that was totally white—the walls, the furniture, even the clothes on the man who sat facing him, were the color of ivory.

The man had smiled warmly and waved Victor over to a chair behind a large, white desk. "Welcome to Psycor," he had said.

Victor sat down at the desk. "What is this place?"

"The Intake Processing Center—IPCEN for short. Our job is to log you in and route you in the right direction."

"That's it?"

"Not quite . . . there's the matter of a few introductory remarks. . . ." The man rose and stepped to a point directly across from Victor. "You'll find a plant in your left front drawer . . . would you place it on the desktop, please."

Victor complied, wondering what the potted plant was for.

"Let us assume," the man suggested, "that you are on a top-priority mission to recover information vital to this nation's security, and you have just learned the data is contained on a microdot hidden somewhere in that plant in front of you. Assume further that you have but five minutes to locate it." The man took a stopwatch from his jacket pocket and clicked it firmly. "Find it."

For a moment Victor was unsure whether the man standing in front of him was serious. Then he saw the expression on his face and heard the stopwatch ticking, and he knew the instructions were for real. Frantically he seized the plant, figuring it was some kind of test. Dumping the contents of the pot in a heap before him, Victor sifted through the soil and examined the surface of the flower, but to no avail. Finally he dismembered the plant completely: shredding the blossoms and leaves until, at last, he found the microdot embedded in a section of stem just above the roots. "Did I make it?" he inquired excitedly, waving the tiny microdot aloft.

"Quite so," the man with the stopwatch replied, nodding his approval. "Now if you'll just sweep that debris to one side we'll see how you make out with the object in the right-hand drawer."

The object in the right-hand drawer turned out to be a white rat in a small, wiremesh cage. Victor had worked with such animals in his psychology courses at the university, and he had no difficulty taking it out of its cage and placing it on the clean section of the desk. "What now?" he asked.

"Same instructions as before. You have five minutes to locate the microdot."

"That should be easy . . . there's not many places to hide it on this fella," Victor responded confidently, moving his fingers gingerly over the rodent's body in search of a telltale bump. The confidence didn't remain for long. "I don't understand," he complained after thoroughly examining the rat twice, "it's just not there."

"You're overlooking the obvious."

"I don't follow."

"Maybe this will help." The man reached inside his jacket again, pulled out a thin steel instrument, and tossed it on the desk.

Victor recognized a scalpel when he saw one. "You're kidding," he said, not knowing how to react.

The man glanced at his stopwatch. "You have just over a minute left."

"You're kidding," Victor repeated, the tension evident in his voice.

"What's the matter?" The man acted as if he didn't understand. "You just took that plant apart to find the microdot, why not the rat?"

"But the plant . . . it's . . . it's . . ."

"Alive," the man interjected, "just like your rat there."

"It's not the same kind of 'alive.'"

The man snatched the rat from Victor's hand and squeezed it flat against the desktop. "What you are saying is that 'aliveness' is a state of mind . . . your mind. You think that the rat is 'alive' so you hesitate to dissect it; you don't think the same of the plant, so you treat it like an inanimate object. Now what if I place a plant and a rat in the same category: the same category you reserve for the plant alone?" While he was talking the man picked the scalpel off the desk and held it over the rat's squirming body. "Then I'd have no compunctions about finding that microdot, would I?"

Victor wasn't able to say anything. He simply sat dumbfounded as the man across from him methodically sliced the rat into pieces, examining each bit of flesh until the tiny sphere was located. "Remember that 'aliveness' is a state of mind," he repeated, sweeping the mutilated body off the desk and onto the floor next to the flower pot, ". . . and we can teach you a state of mind." Victor had nodded blankly, but all he could remember thinking was how starkly crimson the rat's blood had appeared spattered against the whiteness of the room.

There was a knock at the door.

Victor reached over and turned off the television. "Marba?" he called out.

"Yes," came the voice from the hallway.

"Just a sec . . ." Victor unbolted the door and motioned for the lieutenant to come in.

"I'm late," Marba announced, "I had to meet with some people." There was an unmistakable tinge of excitement in his voice.

Victor closed the door and followed Marba to the closet. "Sounds like it was a good meeting."

"It was," Marba agreed, hanging up his coat. He rubbed his hands together. "One thing hasn't changed around here—the fuckin' winters. I thought I'd freeze my ass just walking over here."

"Want some coffee?"

"Now that's the first *good* suggestion you've made since you got here."

Victor ignored the dig. There was no way Marba was

going to get to him—not after the mindlock he had placed on his feelings concerning the old man. Besides, the lieutenant was acting almost jovial, and that meant he was being almost bearable. Victor marveled at the way he could change moods, like a cosmolite changed orbit. "There's a pot over on the dresser . . . I'll get some cups from the john."

While Victor was in the bathroom Marba brought the coffee and some napkins to the table near the window. "How about a view of the city while we drink?" he called out.

"Fine by me," Victor agreed, emerging from the bathroom with two freshly washed cups. "One for you," he explained, putting the cups on the table and filling them with coffee.

Marba picked up his cup at once, cradling it just below his chin and letting the warmth and aroma of the coffee play over his face for a moment before he took a sip. "That *is* good," he said approvingly, raising the cup to his lips again.

For several minutes the two men drank their coffee in silence. Victor did nothing to disturb the interlude: even though no words were exchanged, he could sense that Marba was getting ready to tell him something important. He could see it in his gestures, in the expression on his face.

Assessing the way Marba felt, without the need for words, wasn't new to Victor. When he had been very young he'd amazed his parents by guessing their moods and how they felt about things. Once they had even asked a psychologist friend about Victor's uncanny predictions, thinking he might have ESP. The psychologist had informed them that there was no such thing as extrasensory perception, but that Victor was highly sensitive to other people's needs and feelings, and could "read their minds" by observing the way they looked and acted. "Empathy" he had called it—and he'd predicted that Victor's empathetic skills would increase as he matured. The psychologist had been right; so right, in fact, that Victor had been preselected for Psycor on the basis of his Empscore alone.

"I've been thinking a lot about our working together," Marba said, breaking the silence at last. He poured himself a second cup of coffee and settled back in his chair. "About whether you're as good as your record indicates . . ." He dabbed at his cup with a napkin. "About the possibility of finding Helen Stenley alive . . ." There was a pause. "Now there's a good one: what if I bring you onto the case to help find her and you end up endangering her life with that maim-and-kill crap they teach you in Psycor these days?" Marba took a drink from his cup, his eyes never leaving Victor's face. "You'll never understand this—but I want Stenley's safe return more than anything else I've ever wanted in my life."

Victor poured himself another cup of coffee. "Why is she that important to you?"

"Because of what she represents—what she believes in . . . and what she can accomplish."

"You mean her support of the Dregs?"

"Not Dregs . . . human beings . . ." Marba corrected. "That and her belief in the future of New York. If you could see how she has helped us already . . ." Marba's face began to brighten—a wisp of a smile at first that broadened into a wholesale grin, and for a moment it seemed to Victor that the old man's face had recaptured some of the elegance the years had squeezed out of it. "God, a woman like that could save this city."

Marba took a drink from his cup, rolling the coffee

around his tongue before he let it run down his throat. "I spoke with the regional director today," he said after a few moments. "She assured me you understood my command authority. Is that true?"

"It is."

Marba got up and stepped to the window, looking past his image superimposed on the skyline of Manhattan. "Then let's try and put our hard feelings aside and get this case solved." He turned to Victor. "What about it?"

"Okay by me," Victor replied immediately, standing up and extending his hand.

Marba reached across the table and clasped it firmly. "I hope you're as good as they say," he stated, taking something from the inner pocket of his jacket. "I want to show you some evidence that might be worth something."

Victor could sense that his competence would soon be tested. "Evidence not presented at the morning briefing?" he wanted to know.

"Right. Let me show you," the lieutenant announced as he unrolled two eight-by-ten photos and adhesived them to the table in front of Victor. "You recognize the shot on the left?"

"It was handed out at the briefing . . . there's the guy holding the petition. . . ."

"Yes." Marba leaned over beside Victor and pointed to one corner of the photo. "But take a look at the guy standing to his right."

Victor fixed his gaze on the location Marba indicated. "I don't see anything special about him," he admitted.

"Neither did I . . . but I played a hunch," Marba replied proudly. "I had a feeling that maybe one, or both of the guys standing next to the suspect might have been in with him on the kidnapping. So I used a computer scan to examine all filmed footage of Stenley's visit and isolate any individuals who image-matched the two men standing near the suspect."

"Computer profile analysis," Victor said casually.

"You know about it?"

Victor smiled. "We do keep updated on detection analysis. What did you find?"

Some of the wind had gone out of Marba's sails, but he still responded boastfully: "The jackpot. Neither the suspect nor the man on his left received any matchups—but we got three possibles and two probables with the guy on the right. Seems he was following Stenley around from the time she entered the city."

"That's him in the second photo, then."

"Yes, taken at a rally a day before the kidnapping. His back was to the camera this time, too, but we did pick something up." Marba used his finger to trace a circle around a section of the man's hand, which stuck part way out of his overcoat pocket. "The guy is holding onto a gun in there."

Victor bent over until his nose was almost touching the picture. "You're right," he agreed, almost having to squint to see the tiny segment of gun butt peeking out of the coat. "How can you be so sure it's the same man in both photos?"

"The same way that we're going to be able to identify him."

Victor moved his head back so he could see the entire photo in better perspective. For a moment he was stumped as to Marba's plan. There were no identifiable marks on the man: no visible scars, no labels on the coat, no rings on the fingers of the gun hand. But wait a minute! Victor refocused his eyes on the back of the man's neck, just above the line of the overcoat. It was so obvious—

how could it have eluded him? "A Bucunni razor cut," he declared, recognizing the distinctive sawtooth arrangement of hair. "And I'll bet there's not more than a few salons in the city that give them."

"Two . . . I already checked. And," Marba added, "one of my people told me barbers can recognize a client as easily from the back as the front, because they cut each head of hair a bit differently."

Victor studied the photo for a few moments more. "Why wasn't this evidence presented this morning?"

"Because the commissioner doesn't know about it."

"Oh?" Victor raised his eyebrows.

"This is a Psycor job. I told you, I can't risk a bunch of half-trained cops running down my two best leads. Especially when most of the men on the force hate Stenley with a passion and would rather have her dead anyway."

"Did I hear you say *two* leads?"

"I was coming to the second one. At the meeting I attended before I came here . . ."

"Go on."

"One of my informers there thinks he knows of an eyewitness to the kidnapping. Someone who might know something but who hasn't divulged the information."

"Do you know who he is?"

"My source thinks he overheard his name as 'Twenty-four.'"

"What the hell kind of name is that?"

"Code name, probably. Who knows? The guy was also wearing a black bracelet on each wrist."

"Does your informer know where this Twenty-four lives?"

"Central Park."

"East or West?"

"Both—he lives *in* the park. Probably belongs to one of the gangs that scavage and fight there."

"They're allowed to live in there?"

"They can do anything they want, as long as they confine their mayhem to the evening hours. Central Park is a recognized frepoint from sunset to sunrise."

"Frepoint? Like in checkpoint?"

"More like 'free' as in 'free for all.' Frepoints are the only places in the city where no land claims of any person or group are recognized."

"So anyone can go there?"

"Yes . . . at their own risk."

"Who'd want to?"

"Sickies . . . people who want to exercise their violence without legal restraint." Marba poured some hot coffee into his half-filled cup. "You have to understand that in this town violence is like drugs. People get addicted to it—it gets into their blood, and they need more and more to be satisfied. Frepoints are urban arenas set aside for these people so they can batter themselves to death without endangering the rest of the population unduly. Central Park is simply your 'civilized' version of a jungle where people with a high tolerance for violence get their final kicks surviving and destroying on a night-to-night basis."

Victor thought for a moment. "Sounds like Central Park hasn't changed much since I was here."

Marba threw back his head and let out a belly laugh. "Shit! The last time you were here there were a few robberies and rapes in the park—even some murders. But the police patrolled the place around the clock and some citizens even used the park at night. Now each evening at sunset the police get the hell out and stay out—no matter what—and each morning at sunrise, sanitation trucks move in to pick up the fresh bodies."

"All right, there's a difference," Victor conceded, raising his hands in mock surrender. "All I have to do is take a stroll in the park, run across this Twenty-four character, find out what he knows about the kidnapping—if he knows anything—and go from there."

"That . . . and track down our friend with the Bucunni haircut."

"Thanks a lot." Victor fished for a package of mints in his shirt pocket. "I'll need a microcopy of the film the commissioner showed this morning."

"What for?"

"I just want to check some of the frames for clues."

"You got something?"

Victor pondered Marba's question. There was something in the kidnap film that didn't sit right with him, but he couldn't put his finger on it. "I just want to take a look," he answered finally, deciding to keep his suspicions to himself until he'd had time to study the pictures in detail.

"All right . . . I'll get a copy over to your hotel."

"One more thing . . ." Victor found the roll of mints and offered one to Marba. "There's still something I don't figure."

"Oh?"

"You. A few hours ago you wouldn't have trusted me to drive you back to Oasis One—now you're willing to let me track down your two best leads. What gives?"

"A few hours ago I hadn't talked to the regional office or seen you decipher the clues I had uncovered."

"So you *were* testing me. . . ."

"Absolutely. I've never run across a Psycor profile with scores like yours. I had to see for myself . . . especially if I was going to let you work on the case."

"You still could track down the suspects yourself," Victor suggested, taking a mint for himself and putting the remainder of the roll on the table.

"Could . . . but can't." Marba rubbed his hand across his forehead. "I have to follow orders, too."

"What orders?"

"Central Operations decided I'm too indispensable to be risked chasing down clues outside the Oasis."

"Kind of makes one wonder what Central Operations thinks of my worth," Victor observed caustically.

"Your worth has nothing to do with it. The reason C.O. can afford to gamble with you is because you don't have the contacts and information I do concerning the kidnapping."

"I've heard that before," Victor muttered to himself.

Marba either didn't hear Victor's utterance or chose to ignore it. He took a can of microfilm from his pants pocket and placed it next to his coffee cup. "I've got some information we should go over—it might help in locating the two men." He unscrewed the cylinder. "You know . . . I'd much rather have your job than mine. Do you know how hard it is to have to depend on someone else to do a job you know you could do yourself? To have to wait . . ." Marba looked sadly at his younger colleague. "No . . . I guess you wouldn't."

Victor started to reply, but thought better of it. It was obvious to him that Central Operations had come down hard on Marba, and he was pleased by this. It was probably his consistent challenges to the lieutenant's competence that had brought about the restrictions in the first place. Yet he did feel a certain uneasiness about the outcome as he sat across from the old man and sensed his bitterness toward the organization he had founded and served so loyally, and which now denied him the opportunity to use his own resources in saving something he held dear.

It was an uneasiness Victor put quickly out of his mind.

CHAPTER SIX

Near the center of Grand Army Plaza, where, in years past, sightseers could rent a horse and carriage to tour the park, people waited for the elesphere that would take them to the top of Skyscape Observation Tower. There, suspended three hundred feet over the Sheep Meadow, they would spend the evening peering through infrascopes, hoping to catch a glimpse of the carnage below.

Beneath the tower a group of creepers prepared to join in the carnage, a few "old-timers" feigning Kung Fu jabs and phantom blade thrusts to the delight of onlookers who had gathered to watch from across Fifty-ninth Street. Victor studied their crude movements in the gathering dusk, wondering how many would make it through the park.

"You there . . ."

Victor turned to confront a girl who was jogging toward him along the Fifth Avenue restraining wall. "You the guy who wants a tag?"

Victor couldn't suppress a grin. When he had offered fifty bucks to get a guide, he hadn't bargained for the apparition before him: a girl young enough to be his daughter, looking like a crumpled grasshopper in her baggy fatigues and fuzzy moccasins. "Isn't it a little early for recess," he joked.

"Suck it, buster." The girl tossed her head in the air and turned away.

"Hey . . . just a minute."

The girl looked back, eyeing him coldly.

"I did ask for a creeper who knows the park."

"Well, that's what I am . . . so fork over the fifty or chase your own ass around the place."

"You'll have to excuse me," Victor said, shaking his head. "You just don't look like someone who'd . . . uh . . . be in this line of work."

"I do my work just fine," she said defiantly. "I've left a few for the trucks already . . . some as old as you."

"Do I detect a subtle hint of violence?"

"That's what you're payin' to see, mister. I can show it to you or I can give it to you." The girl moved to within a few feet of Victor and stared down at him from her position atop the wall. "So why don't you just fork over the fifty or fuck off," she commanded, extending her hand.

"I want you to help me locate someone," Victor explained, reaching into his pocket.

"Fifty buys you a night in the park, not a detective agency."

Victor pulled out a roll of bills. "How much does a hundred buy me?" he asked, pulling off two fifties.

"The chance to get a detective agency for two hundred."

"You're pretty fast." Victor took two more fifties from the roll and held out the four bills. "Not that fast," he cautioned, gripping the money firmly as the girl tried to tug it from his hand. "What if the detectives don't come through?"

The girl gave a strong yank and wrested away the cash. "You can try and ask for your money back," she challenged, stuffing the money into her knee pocket.

"I'm better at deposits than withdrawals." Victor stood up. "Hey, does the two bills entitle me to a name?"

"It's Reeva."

"All right, Reeva . . . when do we head in?"

"Anytime you're ready," she said, noting that some of the more experienced creepers were already fanning out into the park. "You want a cross or a perim?"

"Come again . . . ?"

"Do you want to cross the park or stay near the perimeter?"

"Whichever is better to find the person I'm looking for."

"Is he a parker?"

"If that means does he live in the park—yes, according to my information. The name is Twenty-four."

Reeva thought for a few moments. "You got a stiff tip. Unless he's a newly, he doesn't stay in Central."

"I got the impression he's been around for a while. You sure you know everyone who's in there?" Victor asked skeptically, pointing toward the park.

"You're goddamned right I do. You think I made it through a thousand crossings knowing nothing?"

"A thousand . . ."

"A thousand plus . . ." the girl corrected proudly. "That puts me in the top fifty for Manhattan. So when I say your friend ain't in there—he ain't."

Victor mulled over his guide's words. "One other thing," he noted, "the guy is supposed to wear black bracelets on both wrists."

"Did you say *black* bracelets?"

"Yes . . . does that help?"

"And the name . . . ?"

"Twenty-four . . . what is it you've got?"

Victor could barely see Reeva's face in the darkness, but he could clearly detect the contempt in her voice.

"It's not Twenty-four . . . it's *Teddy*-four. The fourth one to join that gang of fuckin' perverts."

"You know him then."

"Oh, I do, all right," she said bitterly. "Bill-five and him diced up one of my friends last year."

"I thought that was all part of your little game."

"My friend was already dead." Reeva cursed under her breath. "Teddy-four is a spineless corpse vulture. He lets others do the killing, then he scours the park for bodies to cut up before the trucks haul them away."

"Do you know where we could find him?"

"Like I said—he moves around . . . but the gang usually hangs out near the receiving reservoir."

"Can you take me there?"

"Sure . . . but that means a crossing."

"So what?"

"It's more dangerous than a perimeter trip . . . think you can handle it?"

"I think so . . . you think you can protect me?"

"You!" she mocked. "I've never lost a gaper yet—and for two hundred I could protect an army like you."

"You don't mind me asking how, do you?"

"I can fight . . . and I can dice." Reeva patted a knife sheath hanging from her belt.

"But it's empty," Victor noticed.

"Whatdidya expect? The cops would pulp us if we carried dags outside a frepoint. Mine's niched just beyond the wall. We'll get it on our way in."

"I'd feel better if you had a gun."

"You would," she said, annoyed. "We don't use guns in there, fella . . . we want kicks—hand-to-hand kicks."

"And the guys inside the park?"

"Them, too. Anybody can pull a fuckin' trigger. But

a knife in the gut . . . a foot in the balls . . . that's action."

"*Nobody* carries a gun?"

"I guess they could . . . but what for? Where's the kicks? Hell: gapers pay cash, creepers get diced, and parkers get jagged—because they want action. You get action with a point, not a pistol." Reeva jumped down to the park side of the wall and motioned Victor to follow. "Let's go," she beckoned, moving off to retrieve her knife.

Along the perimeter of the park, the lights from the Oasis cast an eerie illumination over the scarred trees that bent wearily toward the barren landscape. A few hundred yards further in, however, the light dwindled into little shadow fragments, and the park darkened under the starless sky. As he stepped beneath the blackening canopy, Victor could feel the energy percolating in his body, experienced the waves of exhilaration, like strips of pressure, tightening across his chest. What a sensation! Automatically, almost imperceptibly, his body braced for action: it was as if he had become a human magnet with one pole ready to attract the slightest sounds and images; the other prepared to repulse anything of danger.

As they moved deeper into the park, Reeva remained unaware of the changes taking place in the man at her side, and that's the way Victor wanted it. She hadn't been trained to detect the subtle changes in his posture; she couldn't recognize the difference in his respiration rate and muscle tonus. She had learned to fight on the streets of New York, not the practice fields at Psycor academy. Victor had no doubt that she could kill . . . in her own sloppy fashion—flailing away with her knife like a glutton at feast. Yet he pitied her, realizing that she could kill a hundred times and never once know the satisfaction of creating an elegant death.

He pitied Marba, too. The old man thought of killing the way creepers like Reeva killed. That the taking of life could become an artistic ballet of exquisite form and movement was lost on him. Victor could understand why. Before his training, he had shared Marba's bias. Before he had undergone gradient training in Dr. Byer's laboratory, he didn't even think he was capable of killing.

The thought of Dr. Byer brought a smile to Victor's lips. He could still remember his first class with the man —could almost hear his high-pitched voice commanding the trainees to be seated at their individual control panels, could almost see the rows of steelglas ovens with their dull-gray feeder arms underneath.

"We're going to teach you how to kill today," Byer had proclaimed in his falsetto voice, and everyone had had a good laugh about that. Then he activated the mechanical arms and everyone watched, fascinated, as twenty pairs of metal fingers dipped in and out of their overhead ovens. It took Victor a moment to detect what the mechanical arm had left behind. It was, as Byer announced, "a mosquito . . . the kind that spreads encephalitis. Set your control dial at plus-five," he commanded, "and kill it."

There was no resistance to the order, and in a few moments twenty jets of blue flame had immolated the insects as they flew about the ovens.

Dr. Byer voiced his pleasure over what had transpired and, while the mechanical arms inserted new objects into the ovens, he warned that health hazards could be created by rodents as well as mosquitos. "Like the rats being placed in your cubicles," he emphasized. "They are infected . . . set your dials at plus-eight and incinerate."

Again the trainees complied, dispatching the rats in sheets of flame; and again Byer expressed his satisfaction over what he observed.

It was at that moment that Victor spotted the dogs being pushed down a long conveyor belt that ran alongside the ovens. A soundproof barrier erected next to the belt muffled the howls of protest as the dogs were jerked up and into the ovens by the mechanical arms, but the sight of bared fangs was ample proof of the animals' terror and pain.

The sight of the dogs being stuffed into the ovens seemed to heighten Byer's enthusiasm. "Do you see man's best friend?" he asked, pointing to where the dogs were clawing frantically at the sides of their glassed prisons. "Did you know that canines kill our livestock and maim our children?" Byer had stepped between the trainees and the ovens. "They are dangerous," he warned emphatically, "they must be exterminated. Set your controls at plus-fifteen and activate the jets."

At first there was no response. It reminded Victor of his experience at IPCEN a few days before—when the man in the white room had told him to cut up the rat. The trainees looked at each other, at Byer, and back at each other. Then they fidgeted about while the doctor walked up and down among them, glaring menacingly. "So you don't believe me, eh?" he asked, waving his hands in nervous, jerky movements. "You know, mosquitos and rats aren't the only disease spreaders around here. You ever heard of rabies?" Byer thrust his pointed face in front of the trainee sitting next to Victor. "Look at the dog in your cubicle . . . you see that foam around the muzzle? You think that's spit, maybe? A little nervous saliva? You fool . . ." he shouted, his expression more frightening than the dog's in the oven, "God help you if that dog lives to bite someone. Kill it! Now!"

Victor watched as his fellow trainee hesitated, his hand tensed near the control dial.

"Insubordination! I won't have it," Byer yelled impatiently. "You . . . all of you . . . burn those dogs or I'll open the ovens and let 'em rip you apart." He turned and moved to the near wall, where a screened enclosure surrounded a series of levers.

The trainee next to Victor had seen enough. He spun his control dial to plus-fifteen and jammed down the "on" button. Instantaneously a massive bolt of flame filled one oven, incinerating the dog inside like it was a wad of paper. The other trainees, including Victor, had also seen enough. They followed the first man's lead, and within a minute the other nineteen dogs were reduced to ashes.

Stepping away from the wall, Dr. Byer became satisfied again. "Very good, gentlemen, *very* good," he exclaimed, slapping his hands together. "Whoever selected you did a good job—it's obvious that you can kill . . . and yet you hesitate to do so unless there is good reason. That's excellent. The first rule you have to learn here is that one kills only when there is good reason to do so." Byer turned so he could smile at the trainee whom he had chastised so severely just a few minutes before. "The second rule you learn is that when there is a good reason to kill, you kill quickly and cleanly. By that I mean swiftly —with no mess. Like the way you killed your dog: you didn't singe it until it died of heat prostration, you blasted it into oblivion with one massive flame."

Byer paused for a moment and then stepped toward the door. "That's all I want to do today," he concluded. "Tomorrow we'll teach you more about how to kill." With that he left the room, leaving Victor and the other trainees to mull over his final comment. Nobody had laughed about it this time.

They had just passed beyond the old Delacorte Theater when Victor heard the sound. It was exquisitely soft —hardly more than the murmur of a twig breaking nearby, but it was enough to bring him to a total halt. His female guide had missed the sound completely, but Victor's sudden break in stride alerted her that something was happening.

"What is it?" she whispered.

Victor never got a chance to answer. From out of the darkness two shadowy figures were already hurtling his way. Had he not stopped short the instant before, they would have crashed directly into him—instead, their momentum sent them careening past and into a row of shrubs some ten feet beyond. One of the attackers seemed to ricochet off the bushes, spinning sideways and stumbling off into the darkness.

His companion wasn't so lucky. For a moment he became entangled in some branches, and in that moment Reeva bolted forward, driving her shoulder full into his midsection with telling force. He doubled over and onto the ground, with Reeva on top of him. Victor, watching the scene with some amusement, suddenly anticipated what was about to happen and tried to intervene.

Too late. Even as the unknown assailant rolled about, trying to catch his breath and shake Reeva loose, she raised her knife and stabbed him through the chest—once, twice, three times, until he lay still. Then she calmly jammed the blade through his head, temple to temple, wiped it clean on the grass, and jammed it back into its sheath.

Victor cursed under his breath. "What the hell did you

do that for?" he hissed, grabbing Reeva by the arm as she got to her feet.

She was obviously surprised by his reaction. "What the hell's the matter with you?" she barked, forgetting for an instant where she was. "Get your hand off my arm," she ordered in a softer, but no less authoritative, voice. "Can't you see that bastard almost killed us?"

Victor glanced at the still form on the ground. A machete lay near one arm. "Couldn't you just have disarmed him?" he wanted to know, still angry. "We might have gotten some information outa him."

"Asshole," Reeva said defiantly. "What kind of durk are you, anyway? I just saved our lives and you're complaining. You just shut your fuckin' mouth and let's get going or you'll be walking out of here by yourself."

Victor returned Reeva's steady gaze with his own. She had spunk, no doubt of that. "How far to the reservoir?"

"Two . . . maybe three blocks," she answered impatiently.

"Just a second . . . I've got an idea."

"We don't have a second. Half the people in the park have probably heard us. Let's get the hell out."

"Will do," Victor grunted, tugging at the lifeless body on the ground, ". . . as soon as I take this parker with us."

Reeva's look of defiance changed to one of disbelief. "What the shit are you doing?" she demanded, stepping in front of Victor as he hoisted the corpse over his shoulder.

"Bringing along some bait to set a trap."

"That's crazy. What if we're attacked with you carrying that thing?"

"I'll expect you to protect us," Victor chortled, winking

at his exasperated guide. "You told me that Teddy-four liked corpses. All right, we're going to give him one."

"You can find him yourself. I'm leaving . . . now."

"It's worth another fifty if you stay."

Reeva balked. "A hundred."

"Fifty . . . unless you carry the corpse."

"Okay, fifty . . . and I hope you bust your balls."

"Did anyone ever tell you that basically you're not a very pleasant person?" Victor inquired sarcastically, pretending to struggle under his burden so that Reeva wouldn't suspect his strength.

Reeva didn't answer. Instead she abruptly strode away, leaving Victor to grope after her in the darkness.

The receiving reservoir where Teddy and his gang supposedly congregated was bordered on its western end by a jogging track and wading pool. It was there that Reeva stopped, crouching behind a stand of trees that fronted the water. "You look a little winded," she chided as Victor caught up with her and dropped his load heavily on the ground.

"Next time you kill," he gasped, bluffing shortness of breath, "pick on someone your own size."

From the expression on her face it was obvious that Reeva was enjoying Victor's feigned discomfort. "Maybe you better rest," she suggested in a show of mock sympathy. "I can finish your job for you."

"I'll finish it," Victor promised, wondering if he could afford to cut his female heckler down to size. "Just tell me where the body should go so Teddy and his friends will see it."

"I'll show you. Think you're ready to move?"

"Go."

"This way." Reeva darted from behind the trees, zigzagged across a strip of open ground, and inched up to a rusted fence that encircled the wading pool. "If you toss the body over the fence . . . there . . ." she whispered, pointing to some old tables near the pool, "you can be sure Teddy and . . ."

Reeva stopped in midsentence. Something had caught her eye. Victor followed the line of her finger to a point just left of the tables. Then he too saw something, barely visible in the darkness. It appeared to be a body.

Reeva began to chuckle softly.

"What's so funny?"

"You . . . carrying that corpse all the way over here— for nothing."

Victor was becoming increasingly annoyed by Reeva's barbs. "Don't be so sure."

"Eh?"

"It could be a trap. It might not be a body at all. And even if it is, Teddy and his gang might have already mutilated it. Then we'd need my corpse, wouldn't we?"

"I still say you broke your ass for nothing."

"Why don't we see about that."

"Fine with me." Reeva began edging along the fence, looking for an opening. She found one about twenty yards from the suspected body, and crawled through. Victor waited a few moments before following, still leery of a trap.

Reeva had already begun examining the object on the ground by the time Victor reached her side. One glance told him, much to his dismay, that the object was a body —and unmarked at that. He knelt down beside Reeva to get a better look. "Aren't you going to say 'I told you so'?" he asked her.

Reeva was suspiciously quiet. "I'm going to have to tell you worse than that," she finally admitted, moving her body to one side so that Victor could get a clear view of the dead man's hands.

Even before he looked he knew. "Oh, shit," he groaned, "you don't mean it."

"Seems somebody beat you to him."

Victor forced himself to look at the dead man's wrists. There was no mistaking the black bracelets on each one. "How can you be sure it's him? Didn't you say everyone in the gang wore the bracelets?"

"Yes—but not everyone looks like Teddy-four. No, it's him, all right. There's no way I'd mistake that face."

"Well, that's just great." Victor let a curse work its way up his throat. "Just fuckin' great." He turned to Reeva, his eyes narrowing. "I suppose you think this is all very funny," he snapped.

Reeva denied the allegation, but there was no mistaking the smug expression on her face. "You wanna take this corpse along, too?" she asked sweetly.

In the time it took his guide to utter the first word of her question, Victor had carefully calculated the degree of the arc his foot would have to travel to drive her right eyeball through its cranial pouch. By the time she had completed her inquiry, he had executed the blow ten times in his imagination.

"Well . . . ?" she prodded, getting no response.

Victor checked himself. "Just get me out of here," he said, a hint of resignation in his voice. It was turning out to be one of those nights.

It was well past 1 A.M. by the time Victor made his way back to the Oasis and down to the Biltmore on Forty-fourth and Madison. Before URDEC, the Biltmore had been one of the numerous New York hotels struggling to stay open in an era of rising costs and dwindling occu-

pancy. Then Oasis One had come along, sheltering the
grand old hotel within its parapets, and in a matter of
months it was filled to capacity. One of the Biltmore's
current guests was T. "Kelly" Richards, licensed real es-
tate broker, amateur horticulturist and suspected hit man
for the eastern arm of the Council. T. "Kelly" Richards
was also the man with the Bucunni haircut who had appeared in Marba's computer profile analysis. It had taken
Victor the entire afternoon to track him down, and now
it was time to ask him some pointed questions.

Richards had a room on the eleventh floor. Stepping
off the elevator, Victor noted the empty corridor with
satisfaction. After the Central Park fiasco, maybe his luck
was turning. Locating Richards' room, he was sure of it:
the unit was at the end of the long hallway, facing a
locked supply cubicle. It was the most isolated room on
the floor, and thus would be the easiest to enter without
drawing undue attention.

Victor took the small vial of Odalarm from his jacket
pocket. Looking at the liquid in the tiny container, he still
found it difficult to believe that just three drops would
turn the entire area into a madhouse—a frenzy of scream-
ing guests tearing frantically from their rooms, stamped-
ing their way to any available exit.

Yet Victor knew it would happen—because it had happened to him. Back at the academy, during a relatively
boring E and E training lecture. One moment he had
been sitting at his desk trying to appear attentive and
then, an instant later, he was tumbling and shoving his
way toward the door while the pungent odor of gas filled
his nostrils and the shrill cry of "gas leak!" filled the air.
It was only after everyone had been reassembled that
Victor and his classmates learned that the entire "emergency" had been a ruse: staged by their instructor to

demonstrate the value of distractions in conducting Entries and Escapes. "The odor you detected wasn't gas at all," he had explained, pointing out that untreated gas was odorless, "it was Odalarm—the component added to gas to give it its unique smell."

Grasping the vial of Odalarm firmly in his right hand, Victor used his left thumb and forefinger to break the security seal, the faint snap barely audible in the silence of the carpeted corridor. Even as he extracted the eye-dropper from the bottleneck the overwhelming chemical scent began fouling the air. "Sixty seconds," Victor reminded himself as he moved quickly down the hallway, squeezing out the few drops of liquid as he went. "Thirty seconds now," he muttered, counting to himself as the fumes slipped through the spaces around and under the apartment doors and into the bedrooms, where dozens of people stirred uneasily in their sleep.

Then the minute was up and Victor sprang into action, racing down the corridor, banging on doors, urging the occupants to "Get out! Get out! There's going to be an explosion!" He pounded on Richards' door last, and then moved a way down the hall to observe the results. If the dossier on "Kelly" was accurate, it would be no easy task to fool him. And if the gas-leak gimmick didn't draw him outside, Victor realized his only choice was to risk the dangers of entering the apartment by force.

Victor didn't have to wait long to see the effects of his handiwork. Up and down the hallway doors burst open, disgorging shouting, harried individuals in all stages of dress. All except for Richards' door, which remained shut, a curiously unyielding barrier in the midst of such frantic activity.

There was a strange sense of unity between Victor and the door he watched so intently. It was a unity of stillness in the midst of velocity. Two fixed points in a universe of movement. There was the elegance of counterpoint in the swirl of human bodies moving freely between the motionless Victor and the motionless door he observed with such intensity.

And then the door began to open. Only slightly at first, an almost imperceptible distance—yet enough to galvanize Victor into motion. The frantic people near him—those who hadn't already made their way to the fire escapes and elevators—were oblivious to his movements.

So was Richards . . . until too late. Convinced, finally, that the fumes in his apartment and the commotion in the hall were for real, he stepped from his room into the hallway. It was there that Victor intercepted him. Richards barely had time to register an expression of surprise before a plus-three impact module smashed into his chest with sledgehammer power, hurling him backward with such force that he literally ricocheted off the wall inside his apartment. Victor holstered his gun and slipped quickly through the open door. Thus far his plan was working to perfection.

The first thing T. "Kelly" Richards experienced upon regaining consciousness was a heavy, dull pain in his chest. The second was the sensation of bindings firmly lashing his hands and feet against a straightback chair.

"What the hell . . ." he said, rolling his head from side to side.

"So you've decided to rejoin the living," Victor observed, stepping from behind the chair into Richards' line of vision. "I didn't think you were going to come around for a while."

Richards stared blankly at the man standing in front of him, a hundred questions stirring in his awakening brain. Victor didn't wait for him to ask any. "I need some information," he explained flatly, "and it would be in your best interest to give it to me."

For a moment Richards contemplated shouting for help as a way to drive off his assailant, but thought better of it when he spotted the pistol in Victor's hand.

"Save your voice," Victor said, anticipating what was going through Richards' mind. "You've been out almost two hours . . . everyone's gone back to bed."

"The gas . . . I remember the gas now."

"There was no gas . . . and now there's no more police or firemen around either . . . so why don't you and I get down to business?"

Richards rocked violently in his chair-prison. "A fucking trick," he hissed, gritting his teeth as he tried to break free of his restraints. "I'll kill you, you motherfuckin' son of a bitch."

"Ah, ah . . . that's not very nice," Victor chided, grabbing Richards by the hair and banging his head against the back of the chair for emphasis. "Not very nice at all. Now you just sit real quiet and answer a few questions and everything will be fine. You understand?" Victor snapped the struggling man's head sharply against the chair again.

"Son of a bitch," Richards gurgled, spitting blood and slumping forward in the chair.

"Listen, you punk, I mean it!" Victor yanked Richards' head back again, but this time he didn't batter it against the chair. "Just tell me who hired you to waste the Stenley woman and we can adjourn this little meeting."

Richards looked glazy-eyed at Victor, blood flowing freely from his ruptured lower lip.

"Don't stall me, fella. I know who you are and what you do. I want that name."

Suddenly, without warning, Richards reared back and

spat at his inquisitor, peppering the front of his shirt with bloody spittle. Then he braced for the expected blow.

It never came. Instead, Victor took some toweling from the kitchen pantry and wiped it across his shirt. "That's your answer, then," he said grimly.

"That's right, cocksucker. You won't get a thing outa me."

"Very admirable—but we'll see about that." Victor checked his watch. "Seems we have the time to see if we can change your mind. Let's try a different strategy," he suggested, moving to one side of his balking prisoner. "Rumor has it you're quite a horticulturist. Am I right?"

"Up your ass."

"Maybe you don't know what the word means. It means you know a lot about different kinds of plants. Right?"

Richards ran his tongue over his puffy lip, saying nothing.

"So you should recognize what this is." Victor reached into his pocket and pulled out a long cucumber.

Richards eyed the vegetable suspiciously, twisting uneasily in his seat.

"What you probably don't know is the relationship between this cucumber and your being tied up here in the kitchen." Victor placed the shiny green vegetable on the counter next to the sink. "Didn't you wonder why you were tied up here rather than, say, the bedroom or even the living room?"

Richards remained silent, his eyes fixed on the cucumber.

"I'll tell you. Because in the Biltmore kitchens they have a little convenience called a disposal, and I want to show you how it works." Victor stepped behind Richards' chair and gave it a shove so that it was flush against the sink. "Now watch this," he commanded, placing one end of the cucumber down the drain and flipping the disposal switch. There was a loud, grating sound and the top half of the cucumber gyrated violently in Victor's relaxed grip. A few seconds later he said: "Let's see what's left," and pulled what remained of the cucumber from the drain. There wasn't much: a kind of sickly grayish pulp, mashed to a point where one could hardly distinguish the seeds from the green outer coat. "Do I make myself clear?" Victor asked.

The man in the chair tried to push himself away from the sink. "Nothing . . . I'll tell you nothing."

"Suit yourself," Victor said harshly, picking up a knife and splitting the cord that bound Richards' right hand to the back of the chair. "Maybe if you lose that green thumb of yours it might loosen your tongue a bit." Victor grabbed his captive's free arm with both hands and forced it toward the drainhole. Richards put up a struggle, but it was useless against Victor's overwhelming strength and leverage. Victor jammed the resisting right hand firmly into the drainhole, down, down, until he could tell the fingers were jammed against the cutting edge of the disposal blades. "One more time . . ." Victor pushed his elbow against the power switch. "Who wanted the Stenley woman dead?"

Richards' face was drained of color except for the dark line of blood running down his chin. He opened his mouth but no words came out.

"Who?" Victor repeated.

"All right . . . all right, goddamnit. Let up on the fuckin' arm."

Victor loosened his grip just enough to allow Richards the chance to move his hand part way out of the drain. "The name . . ."

"Listen, I don't know who ordered the hit—I just followed—"

"Cut the shit," Victor interrupted, jamming Richards'
hand back against the disposal blades.

"It's the truth . . . the fuckin' truth. I got the contract,
but I don't know who put it out."

"Then who gave you the contract?"

"I . . . I . . ."

"No more stalling." Victor increased the pressure on
Richards' arm.

"Bastard!" Richards grunted, wincing with pain. "It's
Stevens . . . Nick Stevens. Now let up, will ya?"

"When you tell me why the Council wanted the Stan-
ley woman dead."

Richards' face reflected an odd mixture of pain and
hate. "You know I wouldn't know that," he rasped, still
trying to wrench his arm free.

"Maybe Stevens might. Where can I find him?"

"I don't know that either . . . we always made arrange-
ments at different places each time."

"You can do better than that." Victor nodded toward
the mutilated cucumber on the pantry. "One last time—
where is this Stevens guy?"

"I tell you I don't . . ." Richards' statement curled off
into a gasp as Victor drove his hand even further into the
unyielding blades. "The domes," he cursed, fighting to
get the words out over the pain and his distended lower
lip.

"Where?"

"The domes . . . on the carrier."

"The pleasure domes?"

"Yes . . . *yes* . . . now let my fuckin' hand alone."

Victor released his hold and watched his victim yank
his hand free of the drain. There were ugly slashes across

the fingers where the blades had cut into the skin. Richards was so intent on examining the extent of his wounds that he failed to notice Victor slipping around behind him. Nor did he see him draw his pistol and set it on maximum kill pressure. It was probably better that he didn't.

An ARC pistol, set at maximum kill pressure and fired at an object within a five-foot radius, leaves very few traces of that object behind. When Victor fired at Richards from point-blank range, his entire head disintegrated as if someone had popped a giant balloon. It was a quick, efficient extermination, the kind Victor liked. And a necessary one, regardless of what Marba believed. He couldn't afford to leave any loose ends around now—particularly if the hunch he was playing turned out to be correct.

The hunch. Victor mulled it over as he deactivated his pistol and wiped down the room. There were some disquieting discrepancies in the Stenley case—and he meant to get to the bottom of them . . . fast.

Outside the hotel a brisk wind was kicking up little eddies of dust along the garbage corridor on Forty-third Street. The chilly air felt good pressing against Victor's face. After enduring indoor stuffiness for three hours, it helped clear his head—helped him think. Think about why the Council wanted Stenley dead. And, more important, think about who wanted Teddy-four dead.

Down on Forty-second Street, just beyond the Oasis perimeter, a detachment of Godsters were staging their sixty-minute revival march through Times Square, beating their kettle drum four times per block to indicate the hour. Victor let his feet wander toward the drummer: down Fifth Avenue, past the South Checkpoint, over the pedestrian causeway, and finally down into New York's only other frepoint. It had been more than twenty-four hours since he'd last slept, yet he wasn't tired. There was a restlessness growing inside him, a bird-dog relentlessness that kept him going when the scent was fresh.

Victor looked about. Everywhere the foulness of Times Square assaulted his senses. It was as if someone had turned a huge sewer inside out, bringing all the human rodents to the surface: the grizzled winos with weary arms scuttling their way to the blood banks; the drawn old women with beady eyes and shopping bags scouring the garbage cans; the urine-soaked drifters hunched into doorways and sprawled over sidewalks. And above it all, the lewdness of stale food and porno magazines stacked in crazy piles behind soot-stained windowglass.

Victor turned away. He had seen enough. New York was a living plague, a mixture of decadence and decay that lay waste to the human spirit. The sooner he finished his assignment and got out, the better he was going to like it.

South Checkpoint was two blocks away. Victor picked up his pace, wanting to return to the Oasis as quickly as possible. He was almost to the mouth of the causeway when a soft moaning sound caught his attention. It came from the narrow corridor of crawlspace between the causeway's support girders. Stopping to investigate, Victor stepped off the sidewalk into the semidarkness of the bleak little tunnel. After the horror of Times Square, he figured he was ready to confront anything. He figured wrong.

The first thing Victor saw was the woman's face. Not even the head of Medusa could have frozen him more effectively in his tracks. What he confronted was so hideous, so overwhelmingly ghastly, that he could only wonder what perversion of nature allowed such a face to exist on a living human being. Even in the half light of the crawlspace it clearly transmitted a sense of untold horror: the eyes, pools of dark terror spilling out of their sockets; the cheeks, or what was left of them, dangling ribbons of pasty flesh where fingernails had raked them from the bone; the mouth, a gaping hole, opened wide as if in midscream.

Victor lowered his eyes. The woman was crouching before him amid the stench of rotting garbage and broken bottles. Although it was near freezing, she wore only a thin cotton dress, which was covered with her own vomit. She was shaking badly, moaning and gasping as her body trembled. Then a violent spasm coursed through her, and as she thrust her hands beneath her tattered dress Victor suddenly understood. He watched, dumbfounded, as she began to tug at the tiny head of a fetus that had appeared in the bloody mouth of her vagina.

Victor had seen enough. He spun around and sprinted to the causeway, shouting at the parapet sentry to summon an ambulance. "A woman's giving birth down there," he gestured frantically, breaking his stride to point in the direction of the crawlspace.

The guard complied, but with little sense of urgency. "It wouldn't be the first time some bitch decided to drop her load in there," he noted, waiting for Victor to reach his station before he casually punched through a call to hospital dispatch. "I hope for her sake she's not a Dreg." The guard noted the puzzled expression on Victor's face. "If she's a Dreg the ambulance crew won't touch her with a ten-foot pole," he explained.

"But why?"

The sentry gave Victor a "you've got to be kidding"

look. "Who the hell needs another Dreg in this city? They're a goddamned human plague already—that's what they are."

"But the woman needs help," Victor argued, catching his breath.

"The city needs help, fella. If those . . ." The guard broke off in midsentence and signaled that someone was on the other end of the line. "I've got another OB in Sewer Lane," he spoke into the receiver, a smile winding its way across his face.

For a moment Victor stood frozen in place. He stared at the man in front of him, trying to fathom what it was that could drive the sentry to such a calloused disregard for human life and suffering. Was it hate? Fear? It was more than that, he decided, it was the city: the effluvia of Times Square, the sadism of Central Park, the doggings in the streets, the frightened faces in the subways—it was all those things mixed together that drained New Yorkers of their human spirit, left them hollow like their Oasis beneath its protective shell.

Marba had talked of saving New York. Saving what? The woman in the crawlspace or the guard that mocked her? Victor had learned to live with death—even to take away life, but not in the way New York did: sadistically, without a reason. Of one thing he was sure: if any entity ever deserved destruction, it was the malignancy called Manhattan.

The guard was still joking on the phone when Victor turned slowly away. "Maybe we should suture their legs together," he was saying. The comment stayed with Victor all the way back to his hotel.

In the eastern sky the first finger of dawn was edging its way over Manhattan, lifting the mantel of darkness

off trees and buildings. In that first light of morning the
white trucks began their methodical search for bodies—
moving like motorized ghosts along the frosted pathways
of Central Park. Every so often a vehicle would roll to a
stop, lower its grappling hook to pluck a lifeless body
from the frozen ground, and hoist it into the jaws of the
disposal drum mounted behind the driver's cab. Then it
would move on in search of more grisly cargo.

The mechanical scavengers had been crisscrossing the
park in search of corpses for almost two hours when the
call went out. One of the drivers had located a major
body cache near the West Portal entrance. By the time
the three other trucks arrived at the scene, a neatly
stacked pile of twenty corpses confronted them. As if by
some prearranged signal, the drivers jockeyed their trucks
into a tight circle around the bodies and began loading
them into the disposal drums. They worked steadily at
their task until the buzzers in their cabs signaled midbreak. Only then did they leave their trucks to inspect
the few remaining corpses on the ground.

By chance the midbreak had sounded just as each
driver completed hoisting a corpse off the ground. That
is where the bodies had been left, and now they hung
from the end of their grappling hooks like landed fish—
swinging ever so slightly above the heads of the drivers,
who sat beneath them sipping beers.

One of the drivers, the man who had uncovered the
pile of bodies, was enthusiastically bragging about his
accomplishment. "That has to be the largest single find
ever," he boasted.

"Don't be so sure of it," one of his coworkers cautioned.
"What about that gang fight near Bethesda Fountain a
few years back?"

"Not a chance," the boastful driver assured him. "I was in on that haul. Fifteen bodies maybe, but no more."

A third driver got into the discussion. "Well, if it is a record, it probably won't be for long. Not the way things have been going lately."

"Meaning . . . ?"

"Meaning that the violence around here is getting worse and it's only a matter of time before the body count does too. Don't be surprised if you find thirty corpses stacked up around here pretty soon."

The boastful driver turned to the one man who hadn't joined the discussion. "Hey, Ted, you think Bill's right?"

Ted took a long draw on his beer. "Probably is," he agreed, using his shirt sleeve to wipe some foam from his lips. "Especially about the increasing violence. Did you catch that dispatch from the Times Square detail on the radio?"

"No."

"One of their drivers found a dead baby in a garbage can a few hours ago."

"A baby?"

"Yeah . . . and just born . . . still had the afterbirth hanging off it."

"Probably a fuckin' Dreg," Bill declared.

"Probably so," Ted agreed, reaching for another beer. "And we have to go around cleaning up after them."

CHAPTER SEVEN

From his position on the observation platform, Victor commanded a clear view of the enormous arena that had housed the New York Stock Exchange before Crimewatch moved in. Looking down, he could see the clusters of people jammed around the communication terminals, could hear the excited voices of citizen volunteers as they reported suspected crime sightings on their individual videophones. Victor smiled. Not much had changed since the crimesighters had replaced the stockbrokers on the huge trading floor below. Even the ticker tape remained, a streamer of letters and figures illuminated against the far wall, except now the symbols identified crimes rather than corporations, and point values referred not to profit and loss but life and death.

"This way, please." An attractive young woman wearing a flashing Crimewatch button motioned for Victor to catch up with the line of people moving toward the floorway entrance. Beside her, two vendors were selling confetti and programs to the visitors as they prepared to pay their admission fees.

"You can't follow the crime without a catalogue," one vendor barked.

"And you can't cheer the crimesighters without your supply of ticker-tape confetti," chimed in the other.

Both men were doing a brisk business.

Victor ignored the two vendors, moving hastily

through the entry turnstile and down the crowded escalator to the cordoned walkway that crisscrossed the entire control complex. Reflexively he dipped his right hand into his pants pocket to protect the small white envelope resting against his wallet. He fingered the corners of the envelope gingerly, feeling the slight bulge from the two microframes sealed inside. It was a pleasant sensation, knowing that they were there. He could hardly wait to show them to Marba, to show the old man once and for all just how birght Victor Slaughter really was.

"Your attention please . . ."

The mechanical voice brought Victor out of his muse and he looked up into the mouth of a loudspeaker suspended a few feet over his head.

"Here are some selected crime indicators after the first hour," the amplified voice boomed out. "Arson, up two; armed robbery, up one; assault, down three; rape, unchanged. Analysts expect crime volume to drop off sometime later in the day due to cold weather conditions. There should be some strength in the robbery group, particularly car theft and home furnishings. Crimewatch wants to thank you for visiting today and increasing the crime interest rate. The next report will be in one hour."

Victor shook his head. It didn't take a great mind to see why crime was the number-one tourist attraction in New York. He looked around. To his left an elderly lady sat stonily in front of her monitor, watching a trickle of pedestrians pass across the screen. If she was aware of Victor, she gave no indication. Her eyes never left the monitor, her hands never strayed from the terminal control board.

Then it happened. Victor spotted it at the same instant the old woman did: a man moving left to right across the lower quadrant of the monitor suddenly darted behind a woman pedestrian, lunged at her purse, and ripped it free.

"ALERT!" The screechy old voice cut into Victor's ears like a fingernail rasping across a blackboard. Below her monitor, the once motionless woman had turned into a human convulsion—arms flying all which ways, torso jiggling, head turning back and forth like a pendulum gone amok. "I've got a live one," she screaked into her videophone. "Monitor 86, robbery, tape mark 0814. Confirm." Even as she spoke a rush of tourists began to push and shove their way to the edge of the walkway railing to catch a glimpse of the excitement.

"Monitor 86, stand by." The image of a police dispatcher materialized on the old lady's videophone. At the sight of the officer she calmed down, staring attentively at his image. "We do have a confirm and a track. Suspect is presently proceeding west along Sixty-third Street and we have projected intercept at the Broadway interchange. You will receive an update." The dispatcher paused for a moment, picked a piece of paper off his desk, and smiled. "Police Central awards you ten-point surveillance credit and a three-hour yellow-grade illuminate for your vigilance."

The old woman beamed. "Oh, thank you," she said proudly as the dispatcher flipped a switch on his terminal matrix. A moment later the opaque cylinder above her monitor began glowing bright yellow. It reminded Victor of the time he hit the jackpot on a Las Vegas slot machine. He chuckled over the memory, turning from the railing to push his way through the throng of tourists who were enthusiastically showering the old lady and her terminal station with handfuls of ticker tape.

That's when Marba spotted him. He had been on the fringe of the crowd and now he moved swiftly down the walkway to Victor's side. "Where've you been?" he asked impatiently, not even saying hello.

"Here . . . you just didn't see me." Victor eyed Marba as he spoke. The lieutenant was rigid, his muscles pulled taut with tension. Only the mouth sagged, as if the corners were being dragged down by the weight of worry and despair. He looked so pitiful that for a moment Victor felt a twinge of sympathy for the old man.

"What did you find out?" Marba demanded, looking about to make sure Victor was the only person listening to his question.

Marba's rudeness made Victor quickly lose his sense of compassion. "I talked to the suspect with the Bucunni haircut," he said curtly. "Have the police turned up any new leads during the night?"

"None. What did he say?"

"No kidnap note?"

"None, damnit. What did he say?"

"The guy's name is Richards—he's a hit man for the Council."

"For the Council?"

"He was going to hit Stenley."

"He said that?"

"Yes. Had a contract out on her."

Marba wrinkled up his face. "It just doesn't make any sense. Why would the Council want Stenley dead?"

"That's what I was wondering."

"Unless . . ." Marba's voice broke off.

"Unless what?"

"Unless the Council thought Stenley was a danger because she could organize the Dregs." Marba scratched at his forehead. "But if the Council sent out a hit man, then who the hell kidnapped her?"

"I was wondering about that, too."

Marba glared at Victor. "Is that all you can do? Wonder? I want answers, damnit! Leads! So now where are we? More questions to answer and not one fuckin' inch closer to Stenley."

"Don't be so sure—the hired killer told me something interesting."

"Why didn't you say so?" Marba snapped, whirling toward Victor.

"You didn't give me a chance."

"For shit's sake, man, what did he say?"

"He fingered the guy who gave him the contract."

"Who?"

"Name's Nick Stevens."

Marba grunted.

"Know him?"

"You bet I do." Marba rubbed his hands together vigorously. "Now we're starting to get somewhere."

"Mind filling me in?"

Marba rubbed his hands some more, a sense of satisfaction filling his consciousness and brightening his expression. "Stevens works for the Council, but he also takes on independent jobs. Maybe the Council didn't take out the contract on Stenley at all—maybe someone else did. We've got to talk to him."

"I figured you'd want to. I found out where we can get a hold of him."

"Good going," Marba exclaimed, genuinely pleased. The feeling of satisfaction that had mellowed his facial expression was now spreading through his entire body, smoothing his gestures and adding an almost jaunty air to his gait. Victor had observed Marba's radical changes in demeanor before, and he watched the present transformation with his usual degree of concern. Any person who could move so rapidly from despondency to elation was probably manic-depressive and certainly unstable. And unpredictable.

"He's hanging around that converted aircraft carrier in the harbor," Victor said.

"The pleasure domes. It figures Stevens would be there—he's a real sex pervert."

"You got a visual on him?"

"Yes."

"Perfect. I'll pay him a visit and get to the bottom of things."

"Hold on." Marba's voice was firm, but the anger and tension had gone out of it. "I'll decide if and when you see Stevens. What else did the hit man say?"

Victor decided it was time to reveal the microframes. "Nothing," he answered, pointing toward an unoccupied restzone, "but I do have something else I think you'll find interesting." Victor stepped off the walkway into a semi-enclosed seating area. "Remember that microfilm of the kidnapping you sent over to my hotel?"

"Yes," Marba recalled, following Victor to a bench in the far corner of the restzone.

"When I got back from questioning Richards, it had arrived, so I examined it. Ever since I saw the film in the commissioner's briefing, something about the kidnapping had bothered me—and it took me two run-throughs to discover what." Victor had to make a conscious effort to keep his voice in check, to keep the pride from spilling in. "It was the ruptured petition bomb found in the police transport. Why was such an important piece of evidence left behind when everything else in the vehicle was so meticulously stripped of clues? Then I noticed this." Victor pulled the small envelope from his pocket.

"What is it?" Marba asked.

"Some important evidence from the film," Victor con-

fided, ripping open the envelope and giving Marba the
two microframes that tumbled into his hand. "The first
frame is of the police officer in the transport, taken a few
moments before he accepted the scroll from the unidentified suspect in the street."

Marba held the piece of film up to the light. "It looks
like he's writing something down."

"His log input. The light in here makes it a little difficult to see. Recognize what's in the second frame?"

"Not sure," Marba intoned, squinting to see the image
more clearly in the diffused illumination.

"It's a blowup of the guard's thumbprint off the undamaged portion of the petition."

"Yes . . . I see that now."

"What about the two frames together. Notice anything
unusual about them?"

Marba examined the two pieces of film one after the
other, passing each frame back and forth before his eyes.
"No," he said finally.

"Any discrepancies?" Victor hinted.

"No, damnit—and I'm not in the mood for games. Just
what the hell is so important?"

"An almost successful deception. See the thumbprint
in the second picture? It's pointing to the right, which
makes sense if you're right-handed." Victor pretended he
was holding a scroll. "See," he demonstrated, "you grip
the top of the petition with the left hand, thumb pointing
east, and roll the paper down with the right. The only
problem is that the guard in the transport was left-
handed. If you look at the first microframe carefully you
can see him making his log entry with his pencil in his
left hand."

Marba stared at the two pieces of film again. "It is amazing," he admitted respectfully. "But why would anybody want to go to the trouble of doing such a thing?"

Victor didn't answer Marba's inquiry. To him it was obvious why someone went to the trouble of creating the deception, as obvious as who was responsible for kidnapping Stenley. But then, he had some information that Marba didn't have: he knew that Teddy-four was dead. Victor thought about the corpse in the park, about the hunch he had evolved to explain the death—even before he had seen the microfilm. It was time to test that hunch now. "I've got a question, too," he told Marba, getting up from the bench.

The lieutenant was watching him closely. "What?" he asked, still puzzling over the microframes.

"It's about that meeting you were at . . . the one where the informer told you about Twenty-four."

"Twenty-four . . . yes . . ." Marba stood up, a mixture of consternation and befuddlement clouding his face. "I was getting to that . . . did you find him?"

Victor's expression didn't change. He knew Marba would ask about Teddy-four, and he knew he would have to lie once he did. The thought of lying didn't bother Victor: he had been trained to lie easily, automatically—in ways which defied detection. Besides, he had convinced himself that such action was vital to the success of his mission, regardless of what Central Operations felt about Marba's authority. What did vex him was the timing of Marba's question—right when he was trying to test his hunch.

"I know where he hangs out and I'll get him tonight," Victor replied confidently, hoping that his optimistic tone would steer Marba back to the original line of questioning.

It didn't work.

"You sure?" Marba wanted to know.

"I said I would." Victor let the impatience show in his voice. "Now, about that meeting . . ."

"All right, but find the guy," Marba demanded. "I don't know how much longer Stenley's got."

"It's as good as done." Victor took a deep breath. "I think it might be wise if I knew who was at the meeting when you heard about Twenty-four."

Marba stepped back and scrutinized Victor carefully, not saying anything one way or the other.

"If anything happens to you, I should have access to those lines of communication," Victor suggested, using an argument he thought would appeal to the old man.

Marba nodded. "I agree," he said.

The comment came as something of a pleasant surprise. Victor had expected a major struggle before Marba would divulge any names.

"I was planning to give you the information," Marba continued, ". . . after I had a chance to see how you'd do last night."

"So, I'm still being tested."

"And will continue to be," Marba promised, "as long as Stenley's life is at stake." He shifted his stance so that he could see Victor and the tourists passing by the rest-zone at the same time. "There were three men at the meeting with me—good informers I've worked with for years. The one who gave me the line on Twenty-four is Lew Elbert, the other two are Mike Lin and Pete Torber."

"Can I get pictures of them?"

"Better . . . you're going to meet them."

"When?"

"Elbert today. He works at Crimewatch, that's why I had you meet me here. Lin and Torber we'll see tomorrow. In the meantime, I've got visuals on all three at the office. You can have them when we stop by to pick up Stevens' mug shot."

Victor gave Marba a satisfied nod of the head. He realized that now was the moment to tender the crucial question. "One more thing . . ." he said casually, "the men at the meeting . . . were any of them Dregs?"

"Two were . . . what of it?"

"Nothing. The central office said you worked with them."

"They're damn right I do," Marba growled, turning toward the restzone entryway. "And Psycor better appreciate how helpful they are."

"You needn't get defensive, I'm sure they do."

"Maybe you should've been around ten years ago."

"What?"

"Skip it." Marba stepped around Victor and back onto the walkway. There was something in the tone of his voice that convinced Victor to take his advice.

Down at the end of the walkway, about a hundred feet from where Victor stood, an autocom panel was suspended over a huge monitor, its message alerting visitors that they were about to view a stop-action rerun of the year's most spectacular crime. Alongside the monitor, a Crimewatch guide was rousingly describing the action on the screen: a gas truck careening wildly down a narrow street.

"In just a few blocks you will catch a glimpse of a massage parlor," she informed the walkway listeners. "One of the women employed in that sex emporium is married to the man you see driving the truck on the screen. He has just discovered where his wife is working and he is mad . . . killing mad. Now . . . there . . . do you see the parlor? On the ground floor . . . a block down on your right."

As the woman droned on so did the truck, more deliberately now—its pace slackening as it swung over toward the curb opposite the side of the street where the parlor was situated.

"Look quickly now," the guide urged the visitors, "because you won't have long to see it." Then she stopped talking and Victor caught a glimpse of the parlor at the same time the truck driver did. A split-screen closeup caught the full fury of the husband's face as he jammed the wheels of his rig hard to the right and sent the vehicle careening across the street and through the plate-glass window of the already crumbling storefront.

For a few brief seconds one could see the terror of it all: the driver's twisted face as it smashed forward against the windshield; the chunks of glass and stone hurtling through the air; the softness of nude bodies tumbling toward the gaping hole that was once a doorway, and then the sheet of flame that enveloped everything in one seering moment of total immolation. Then the screen went dark.

The guide began speaking again. "Now let's take a look at a slow-motion rerun of the same crime," she said.

Victor didn't wait around to watch.

CHAPTER EIGHT

As the hovershuttle skimmed past the Statue of Liberty, very few passengers paused to take notice. They were too preoccupied with thoughts of sex and gambling, too busy poring over the deck directory of the ship they were about to visit.

Victor too ignored the Statue of Liberty, but his mind was on his work. Standing on the bridge of the hovershuttle, gazing out at the converted aircraft carrier looming massively over the bow, he thought about his kidnap theory and the evidence he had amassed suggesting that Stenley had collaborated with the Dregs in planning her own abduction. It wasn't a theory that would endear him to Marba: the old man was so fanatically loyal to the woman that there was no telling what he might do if her virtue was challenged, let alone destroyed. Yet soon he would have to be told of her involvement in the kidnapping, and that meant Victor would soon have to do the telling.

It wasn't a very pleasant prospect. Already Victor had imagined five or six possible ways the confrontation might develop, and they all turned out the same . . . extremely undesirable. It wasn't very difficult for him to predict the course of the conversation.

He would begin by suggesting that Stenley and the Dregs had plotted the kidnapping together.

Marba would respond with laughter and ridicule.

Then he would present their motives: free national publicity; a chance to rally public support for their cause; even the opportunity to elicit congressional outrage if people began believing that lax law enforcement played a role in the crime.

Marba would stop laughing and start scoffing, chiding Victor for being so stupid.

At that point he'd begin detailing the hard evidence. He'd speak of Teddy-four's death and how it had occurred after Marba's Dreg friends had learned from the informer that he knew something about the kidnapping.

Marba would become a bit more harsh, claiming that the whole thing was mere coincidence and to stop wasting his time.

Then the issue of the doctored thumbprint would be raised.

Marba would become very quiet.

It would be explained how the thumbprint had been planted to throw the police off course. How the man who had approached the police cruiser and the petition he'd carried were both decoys, designed to shield Stenley from suspicion. How the real armed petition was already in the cruiser, in Stenley's possession. How she'd activated it at the right moment and taken a short nap while her associates moved in, placed the detonated scroll in the guard's hand, and removed her and the decoy scroll from the vehicle. How they'd taken off—leaving behind the visual setup they hoped would put them in the clear.

At this point Marba would become belligerent. He would threaten and curse, possibly even become violent.

It wasn't a very pleasant prospect. Victor had seen Marba in a foul mood before and he had no desire to witness one again. Yet, considering his obsession with Stenley—an obsession that cost him his objectivity and blinded him to her faults—it was likely that such an outburst would occur. It was too bad, Victor thought, too bad Marba couldn't appreciate the bright side of the kidnapping: the fact that if Stenley hadn't arranged for her own abduction she probably would already be dead, killed on contract.

The thought of a contract turned Victor's attention back to the present and his anticipated meeting with Nick Stevens. If he was in the domes, like the hit man Richards had claimed, then the meeting wasn't far off. Already the hovershuttle was making its final approach to the carrier, its stubby nose edging toward the huge vessel's entlock.

Pausing for a moment on the massive flight deck, surrounded by crap tables and cat houses, it was difficult for Victor to imagine that men had fought and died where he now stood. But then, not many aircraft carriers had been taken out of mothballs, been completely refurbished, rechristened Pleasure Island, and turned into a floating Elysium.

"She's a beautiful ship, ain't she?"

Victor turned to confront an elderly man waving at him with a carved wooden walking stick. He was wearing a bright red double-breasted sportcoat with an American Legion button over one pocket. "You been aboard before?"

"No," Victor replied curtly, in no mood to talk with the pushy stranger.

"Well, better late than never, I always say," he chuckled, oblivious to Victor's cold shoulder. "I live below," he announced proudly.

Victor eyed the old man suspiciously.

"Yes, sir, cabin 1942. That's the year I served on this ship. Pacific Theater it was. Got three Jap planes right off that turret over there." The man pointed in the direction of two ack-ack guns, their muzzles barely protruding from the top of a golden-shower pleasure dome.

"How long have you lived on board?" Victor asked, a twinge of interest in his voice.

"Almost three years now. Yep, and I've been in almost every dome, too."

"Then you probably know where everything is located on the ship."

"Indeed I do." The old man took a chamois from his pocket and began rubbing the silver heel of his walking stick. "You gonna get some tail?" he asked brightly.

"Not exactly."

The old man looked disappointed. "They've got the best ass in the world here, you should try it." He thought for a moment. "You're a gambler, then."

"Not exactly that either."

"Well, what *are* you here for then?"

"I'm looking for someone."

The old man gave a final vigorous swipe across his stick, inspected the sheen, and tapped it smartly against the heel of his shoe. "Well, I hope you find him," he said offhandedly, pocketing his chamois and turning to walk away.

"Just a moment." Now it was Victor's turn to sound enthusiastic. "Maybe you can help me."

The old man held up. "Listen, mate, not meaning to sound unfriendly or anything . . . but if you wanna find someone, pick up a house phone and they'll page him for you. Me . . . I'm looking for someone who wants to do a little whoring."

Victor took a hard look at the elderly gentleman in his colorful sportcoat. From an engineering standpoint, he just didn't seem designed to endure the rigors of genital

contact. Frail and obviously aged, he appeared suscepti-
ble to pulverization if his partner turned passionate.
Then, too, there was the problem of consummating the
sex act: the old man's outward appearance didn't hold
much hope for a turgid penis tucked between his spindly
legs.

"What's the matter?" the old man asked defensively,
aware that Victor was staring at him. "Something wrong
with wanting to get your rocks off?"

"Nothing like that," Victor assured him. "I was just
thinking that maybe we can get some action together after all."

"Hey, now you're talkin'. I know some great domes—
they're over on B deck. They'll give you—"

"Hold it," Victor appealed. "I already know the dome
I want to go to."

"Why didn't you tell me? What's the name?"

"That's the problem. I'm not sure."

The old man raised his eyebrows. "Not sure?"

"That's right. The guy who recommended the dome
didn't tell me the name of it."

"So what good does that do?"

"Maybe no good . . . maybe a lot of good." Victor
reached into his pocket and fished out the mug shot of
Nick Stevens, which Marba had given him. "The guy
visits here all the time," he said, holding the picture out.
"Maybe you've run across him and know the dome he
visits."

The old man ignored the photo. "You think I'm a fool?"
he asked angrily, scowling at Victor. "You just want to
find that guy."

Victor snorted. "If I thought you were a fool, I
wouldn't have shown you the picture." As he spoke he

rotated the photo slightly in his hand, exposing the corner of a fifty-dollar bill nestled behind it.

The old man's eyes bulged. "I guess I was a little hasty there, mate. Let me see that picture close up."

Victor handed him the picture and the money.

The man took one look, shoved the bill into his pocket, and chuckled to himself.

"Well?" Victor prodded.

"You got a real winner there, son. A real ass man." He handed the picture back to Victor.

"You know him then?"

"Him . . . and the dome he hangs out in. Only uses one."

"Let's go then."

"All right . . . if you're sure."

"I don't get you."

"It's the dome you want to visit. . . ." The old man studied the carved head of his walking stick, turning it over slowly in his hands. "It caters to freak parties."

"Perversions?"

The old man laughed. "There's no such word out here. Anything is normal, for a price. But the dome you're going to: it's not for beginners."

"I think I can manage," Victor countered tersely, catching the innuendo in the old man's comment.

"Suit yourself." Victor's hired guide stepped smartly onto the gangway, tapping the metal deck of the carrier with his polished stick as he walked.

There was no wasted space on the flight deck of Pleasure Island. Foot for foot, yard for yard, it contained more hedonistic delights than any other adult playland in the world. Next to Oasis One, it was New York's biggest tourist attraction, and as Victor made his way between the translucent domes he could understand why. Lust had not been left to chance on Pleasure Island. Every sexual urge, every carnal desire that could be imagined could also be fulfilled somewhere on the huge ship . . . for a price. The same was true for gambling. If one could imagine a wager, chances are he could make it in one of the numerous casinos or outdoor gaming areas ringing the carrier.

The pleasure dome that Nick Stevens frequented was off at one end of the flight deck, nestled in a cluster of old-time saloons and pizza parlors. It was the largest dome in the vicinity, rising a good forty feet into the air, and it glowed with a pulsing red light that seemed to emanate from the walls of the structure itself.

Arriving at the entryway of the illuminated dome, Victor's guide gestured toward the young woman waiting near the sliding door panels. "She'll take care of you," he explained. "This is where I get off."

"You're not coming with me?" Victor wanted to know.

"No. I got other plans."

"It's not too advanced for you, is it?" Victor taunted, taking the opportunity to get even with the old man for his earlier observation.

The old man took a while to answer. "Not at all," he said finally, "I just feel like watching an animal show tonight."

"All right then," Victor waved, satisfied that his barb had found its mark. "Thanks for the help."

The old man nodded and shuffled off, his walking stick tucked tightly under his arm. For a few moments Victor watched after him, then turned to confront the woman standing at the pleasure dome entrance. She was not what he had expected. Strikingly attractive and regally dressed in a formal white gown, she just didn't fit his stereotype of how a prostitute should look.

The girl moved her lips ever so slightly, just enough to reveal the beginnings of a suggestive smile. "Want to try a little tunneling?" she murmured, the words seeming to float from her mouth on little wisps of breath.

It didn't take Victor long to decide. "With you I'll try anything," he enthused, stepping forward and taking her by the arm. He was beginning to think that interrogating Stevens wouldn't be such a waste of time after all.

The woman fixed him with an inquisitive look. "You've never been here before, have you?"

"No, why?"

"Because I'm only a hostess. I don't work on the inside."

"I should have figured," Victor replied gruffly. "A good-looking come-on. I can imagine what the stuff inside is like."

"What's inside is just as sharp as I am," she cooed reassuringly, nudging Victor toward the door panels a few feet away. "If you don't like what you see, you don't have to pay."

"Sounds fair," Victor had to admit, still disappointed that the hostess wasn't part of the package.

"Then in here, please." The woman used her free arm to motion toward the door panels, which were edging open. Victor complied, stepping through the entryway onto a carpeted walkway that edged around the periphery of the dome like a track around a football field. A high wall, inset with numerous doors, bordered the right side of the walkway and prevented Victor from seeing what lay beyond. "Just a little further," the woman promised invitingly, leading Victor some fifty feet down the narrow corridor before she stopped to open a door marked with the letter P.

Victor peered inside. There wasn't much to see: the room was postage-stamp size and sparsely furnished with two chairs, a small table, and a shower stall. It was vaguely reminiscent of Marba's office, except the furniture was newer. He walked in, followed by his female companion, who shut the door firmly behind her.

Once inside the room, Victor lost no time speaking up. "I've got a question to ask you," he told the woman, reaching into his pocket for the photograph of Stevens.

"We'll have to check you first," she insisted. Her tone suddenly seemed more businesslike. "Do you have your VD immunization card?"

Victor pulled out his billfold. "It's here somewhere," he assured her, thumbing through his papers for the small plastic document. He found it wedged between his driver's license and identiplate. "Here you go," he said, handing it to her.

She studied it briefly and started to frown.

"What's the matter?"

"The date you got your last shot. It's been over a year."

"Here, let me see that." Victor reached over and took back his card.

"Oh, c'mon," he complained, double-checking the date, "it's been just under thirteen months."

"You're supposed to have a booster every year."

"Supposed to, but the shot is good for at least eighteen months, and you know it."

"That may be, but between twelve and eighteen months we have to check you ourselves."

"What the hell for? The last shot is good, I tell you."

The woman was adamant. "Either I check you or you don't go in the tunnels."

"All right. All right—check me." Victor undid his belt and pulled down his trousers and underwear in one deft movement. "Just go easy."

"Over here," she ordered, sitting down on one of the wooden chairs and motioning Victor to stand in front of her. "That's right," she nodded, reaching out to milk his penis with her right hand. "How much do you want to spend?" she asked, bringing her left hand under Victor's balls and rubbing while her right hand kept pulling.

"This is worse than a medical checkup," Victor complained, in no mood to talk prices.

"Just relax," she said, using the tip of her thumb to spread open the hole at the tip of his cock. "You're all right," she said, wiping her thumb on her dress. "Now, how much can you spend?"

"What's available?"

The woman bit at her lower lip. "Do you know *any-thing* about the tunnels?"

"Not really."

"Okay, I'll explain them to you," she said, pointing to the chair across from her and motioning for Victor to sit down. "You ever slept in a waterbed?" she inquired.

"Yes."

"Well, our tunnels begin where waterbeds leave off. Anyone can lie on a waterbed, but in our tunnels you can lie *in* one: be totally surrounded by soft, pliable, synthetic membrane that is warm and moist to the touch. Imagine how nice it will feel to crawl through such a passageway, to fuck in such a passageway."

"I'm imagining," Victor assured her, "I'm imagining."

"There are vibrators built into the tunnel walls, too," she added. "In some sections you can just lie on your back or stomach and be carried along on the membrane."

"Peristalsis, eh?"

"What?"

"Never mind. How much does it cost?" Victor could feel a restless urge stirring in his balls.

"That depends on how long you spend in the tunnels and which tunnel complex you choose to enter."

"There's more than one?"

"Right: a 'one-way' tunnel for heterosexuals, and a 'two-way' tunnel for people who go both ways. Tunnel time is fifty dollars for the first thirty minutes and one dollar for each minute after that."

"So I can get in for fifty dollars."

"Not quite—you've forgotten the tunnel fee."

"I can see you don't believe in free love," Victor grumbled.

The woman shot him a dirty look.

"Listen, forget what I just said." Victor reached into his billfold and handed her two fifty-dollar bills. "What'll that buy me?"

The woman's eyes brightened and the sweetness returned to her voice. "Thirty minutes and total tunnel access."

"Total tunnel?"

"The right to visit both tunnel complexes. It costs thirty dollars to visit either tunnel separately, so you're saving ten dollars on the deal."

"What's to stop someone from sneaking into a tunnel he didn't pay for—or going into the wrong one accidentally, for that matter?"

"The sensor band you'll be wearing." The woman walked over to the small table, rummaged through the top drawer, and took out a broad metal cuff. "We lock this on your wrist before you enter the Tunnelarium," she explained, handing the cuff to Victor. "There's a sensor device inside that picks up signals from the tunnel walls and determines if you're in the right passageway. You've got a total tunnel bracelet with a sensor that accepts both one-way and two-way tunnel frequencies; but if a person with a one-way bracelet tried to go in a bisexual tunnel, his sensor would activate an alarm signal, warning him to stay out."

"How loud is the signal?"

"It's not a noise, it's a vibration. The sensor activates a vibracrystal on the bottom of the bracelet that buzzes against a person's wrist."

"Clever," Victor acknowledged, turning the cuff over in his hands. "But why shouldn't a guy just ignore it and go into the tunnel anyway?"

"Because at the same time the sensor alerts him it also alerts us. If the person continues into the tunnel we send out security to get him."

"And this spot on my cuff . . ." Victor noted, pointing to a tiny grid on the bottom of his bracelet, "is it a vibra-crystal?"

"Yes. But it's attached to the timer on the front of your cuff. It signals you when your thirty minutes is up. As soon as we lock your bracelet on, your timer begins."

"Does security—"

"Wait," the woman interrupted, "no more questions, please. If you'll just get undressed and shower I can oil you down and get you into the tunnels so you can see things for yourself."

"Just one more question?"

"One more," she agreed reluctantly, "but start getting undressed."

Victor reached into his pocket and produced Nick Stevens' photo. "Do you know which tunnel this guy hangs out in?"

The woman recognized the face in the picture immediately. "Both . . . he goes all over."

"Thanks," Victor said, handing her a ten-dollar bill.
"Now how about that oil job?"

She took the money and grinned broadly. "Just get
those clothes off and shower and I'll lubricate you so well
you'll float down those passageways."

Victor didn't need to be urged twice.

At first glance the Tunnelarium reminded Victor of a
giant block of swiss cheese. As large as a house, it rested
massively in the center of the dome, a configuration of
gaping black tunnel-mouths bathed in an eerie blue-
green light. For a while he just stood staring at it, then
he walked over and boosted himself into a passageway
some four feet off the ground.

It was like climbing into a warm, wet sponge, but
softer, so very much softer. And alive! Victor could sense
the walls pulsing, breathing in and out around his body;
could feel the damp membrane as it touched the moist
oiliness of his own skin. It was an exhilarating sensation;
and for a moment Victor let his mind go blank, thrusting
his naked body deeper into the darkened passageway.

That's when it happened. Victor plowed headlong
into an obstacle and for an instant he thought a section
of tunnel had collapsed, blocking the way with a chunk
of membrane wall. Then his hand brushed over the hard-
ness of a nipple and he knew the barrier was human.

The woman didn't make a sound. She just twisted over
and clamped her body firmly against Victor's. It was a
weird feeling, being encompassed by organic flesh and
synthetic membrane at the same time, and Victor wasn't
always sure which was which—but he certainly wasn't
complaining. He licked and thrust with abandon, embed-

ding his tongue and cock into any object resembling an orifice, succeeding finally in locating his vaginal target. His partner let out a long, low sigh and banged her hips against the undulating tunnel floor. The recoil sent them both careening off the ceiling. Hurling about the passageway, rebounding off the walls with increasing velocity, the interlocked couple tumbled toward orgasm. The woman was moaning now, little sob-groans that spilled out on shallow gasps of breath. Victor was concentrating too hard to moan, valiantly attempting to synchronize his penile thrusts with the collision rhythm of his body against the floor and ceiling of the tunnel. It was like trying to land a jet on a carrier during a thunderstorm. Just when he thought his balls would explode with pressure, he harmonized stroke with counterstroke, thrusting downward at the exact moment his partner was catapulting off the tunnel floor. Belly slapped loudly against belly and the length of Victor's penis spiked its way into her steaming, slippery crevice. The woman wailed, thrashing her pelvis about, and Victor could feel the ring of vaginal muscle tighten around the head of his cock, could feel it move in a wave down the shaft. He came then, great bolts of sperm driven from his balls in spasms of thrust and recoil. His partner came too, arching her back to contain the surging inner tremble that flooded from her clit to the pit of her stomach. Then she collapsed heavily to the tunnel floor, sighing at the warmth that radiated up from her abdomen.

It was several minutes before the tunnel walls stopped reverberating and Victor opened his eyes. For the first time he became aware of a soft light illuminating the immediate area. It came from within the tunnel walls, and he suspected that it was triggered by a heat sensor. Certainly things had turned warm in his portion of the passageway.

Victor glanced down at the girl lying motionless in his arms. She wasn't that attractive and he guessed she was probably a visitor like himself, not a pro. He started to say something and then noticed that she was breathing rhythmically with her eyes closed. "Just like a woman to turn over and go to bed," he grumbled to himself, tugging his arms from beneath her back and moving off down the passageway. Twenty minutes later he spotted Nick Stevens.

It happened in the two-way passage. Victor had just entered the complex after paying fifty dollars for additional tunnel time when he noticed a faint glow off in the distance. He moved toward it, reasoning that where there was light there was life. Edging closer, he began to suspect just how much life was involved—no two bodies could generate the heat necessary to trigger the illumination he was encountering.

Maneuvering around a sharp bend in the two-way tunnel, Victor abruptly reached the light source, a section of passageway crammed full with people—fifteen, maybe twenty persons jumbled together in one squirming pile. He approached the tangle of bodies gingerly, trying to keep his balance in the heaving, pitching tunnel. Arriving at the periphery of the human roadblock, he could readily tell that he was in the bisexual passageway: in the orgy unfolding before him, partners were chosen by propinquity rather than gender.

Victor waded into the heap of bodies in search of Stevens. It wasn't an easy quest, trying to stay on his feet while he scrutinized faces often obscured by shadows or other bodies. Twice he steered his way through the human entanglement to no avail. Stevens just didn't seem to be there. Then, on a third passage, he slipped and fell among the undulating bodies, his nostrils filling with the musky-pungent odor of sperm mixed with vaginal lubricant. The heady aroma perked his sexual appetite anew and he interrupted his probe to bury his head between the nearest person's loins, not knowing whether he would have to suck or lick, and not really caring.

It was a while before Victor emerged from the orgy, his energy noticeably flagging. Checking his wrist timer, he noted that only a few minutes of tunnel time remained. And still no sign of Stevens. He swore roundly and struck out through the tunnels again, angry that Stevens had eluded him and disgusted with himself for the time he had lost fucking around.

Victor was almost to the end of the two-way tunnel complex when he heard the voices. They seemed to come from the walkway ringing the Tunnelarium, and he hustled to the mouth of the passageway to take a look. He arrived just in time to catch a glimpse of two men as they passed by him on the way to the changing rooms. Nobody could blame Victor for doing a double take. That one of the men had been Stevens was reason enough for surprise. Yet it was the man next to him that presented the greatest potential for bewilderment. Victor had seen the man once before. In a photograph. A photograph he had received from Marba. And Victor never forgot a face —particularly that face, the face of Mike Lin, one of the Dregs he was scheduled to meet the following day.

What the hell was he doing with Stevens? That's what Victor didn't know, and that's what Victor intended to find out . . . fast.

CHAPTER NINE

The traffic coming off Battery Park onto the West Side Highway was heavy enough to shield the movements of Victor's cab and he was thankful for that. A few cars ahead, Mike Lin was maneuvering his battered pickup truck into the center lane, sticking his arm out the window to signal his intentions.

"Keep with him," Victor prodded his cabbie, "there's twenty in it for you if you stay on his tail."

"Don't you worry, mister," the driver barked into his speakercom, "for twenty dollars I can follow a fuckin' snowflake through a blizzard."

He was right. All the way uptown the electric taxi moved silently, flawlessly after its quarry, as if it were linked to the truck by some invisible tow line. It was only when the pickup turned off Ninety-sixth onto Amsterdam that the cab broke pace and the driver asked Victor: "You sure you want to go in here?"

Victor waved him on. He certainly didn't want to lose Lin now, not after he had skipped questioning Stevens so that he could trail the Dreg off the pleasure ship. "What's the problem?" he asked.

"Lota Dregs around here. And it's not very well patrolled."

"Forget it . . . just keep following."

"I don't know . . . some cabs have gotten fucked over around here before."

Victor could see the cabbie's face in the rear view mirror and the expression wasn't very optimistic. "I'll give you twenty more bucks if you go on," he bargained.

The face in the mirror changed. "You got yourself a deal," the driver agreed, renewing his pursuit of the pickup truck. "But pass the money up this way now . . . just in case anything happens."

"Here." Victor stuffed two twenties in the steelglas cash tray and shoved it shut. "Any idea where he might be heading?" Victor gestured in the direction of the truck.

"Yeah. There's a big wrecking yard about a mile from here—he's probably headed there."

"Why there and no place else?"

"There is no place else." The cabbie turned in his seat to catch a glimpse of his passenger. "This whole area is being torn down—from Ninety-eighth up through Morningside Heights. Nothing but abandoned buildings and Dregs left around here anymore."

"And the wrecking company?"

"Paid by the city to level the place. And get this: the fuckin' place is owned by Dregs." The driver lowered his windowshield, cleared his throat noisily, and spit a mass of phlegm into the street. "Some fuckin' deal, eh? Goddamn Dregs get welfare to live up here in the first place and then they get more fuckin' money to tear the place down."

"The city could award a contract to some other firm."

"That's a good one!" The driver wiped his shirt sleeve across his mouth. "If any other wreckers tried to go in there the Dregs would pick 'em off. Those bastards can . . ." The cabbie cut his statement short and squinted intently out his windshield. "There . . . whaddid I tell you," he said, pointing down the road where the pickup truck was turning into a rubble-strewn driveway. "That's the rear entrance to the wrecking yard."

"Just drive by and don't slow down," Victor instructed, lowering his head so he could see out the windshield more easily. "That's the name of the place?" he asked, spotting a large wooden sign fronting 108th Street.

"Yup. Tork Wrecking. Big motherfucking place, ain't it?"

"Looks that way," Victor concurred, noting the rows of ramshackle warehouses and heaps of scrap metal that ran on for blocks behind rows of barbed-wire fencing. "Pull up on 114th and I'll get out."

"Hey, man, by yourself? That's crazy."

"I'll be all right, just do as I say."

"Okay—it's your life." The driver pulled over to the curb, scrutinizing the deserted sidewalk for any possible signs of trouble. "That'll be eight dollars and sixty cents."

Victor put ten dollars in the cash tray and opened the rear door. "Drive carefully," he said, winking at the cabbie who watched him depart in silence, a look of incredulity stamped on his face.

Looking east along 114th Street, Victor found it difficult to believe that commerce and residential life had once flourished there, that the lifeblood of the city had once stirred there. Now the crumbling shells of broken buildings lay like shattered bones on the littered ground, the lifeblood that sustained them turned to powder, eddies of red mortar dust swirling along the gutters.

Victor walked amid the desolation for several blocks, putting his mind in order and searching for the reason why a Dreg who supposedly revered Stenley would be meeting with a Council middleman who ostensibly wanted her dead. Maybe Lin was working both sides of the fence, or possibly he was a Council operative all along. Maybe the meeting was purely coincidental and had nothing to do with Stenley at all. Maybe. The problem was that there were too many "maybes" when Victor wanted a "for sure." And the best place to find that "for sure," he reasoned, was on the other side of the crudely strung barbed wire, inside the Tork Wrecking Yard. Dusk was already casting shadows along the length of the street when he bolted over a sagging portion of the barrier, dived forward, and pressed himself flat behind some rusting girders on the other side. There he waited until evening absorbed the twilight and he could venture forward under the cover of darkness.

Victor knew precisely where he wanted to go. Edging out from behind the pile of girders, he zigzagged his way across a rubble-strewn dumping zone toward a sodium arc beacon some five hundred yards away. The beacon cast the only illumination over the entire yard, a harsh metallic glow that seemed to oxidize the air, coloring it reddish-brown like the rusted hunks of iron and steel strewn over the ground.

Directly beneath the light tower was Victor's objective: a sprawling Quonset hut that stretched for nearly two city blocks. It was the largest, most fully illuminated structure in the area and, Victor assumed, the most likely place to start seeking clues to Mike Lin's behavior. He moved to within two hundred feet of the building without incident, crouching low to the ground to avoid detection.

Then, abruptly, he stopped. Had he heard a noise? A whining sound? He couldn't be sure. He listened for several seconds . . . nothing. It didn't make him breathe much easier—looking about, he realized that the final steps to his destination would be the most dangerous:

over an open section of paved road which ran from the wrecking yard entrance to a bowl-shaped parking area fronting the Quonset hut. Huge mounds of wrecked automobiles lined both sides of the roadway, leaving just enough room for two lanes of traffic and, possibly, a concealed gunman.

Victor readied himself for possible assault control and stepped onto the pavement, staying close to the line of scrapped cars to take full advantage of the protection and concealment their bulky metal bodies afforded. It turned out that the assault preparation was unnecessary as he reached the Quonset hut without incident; yet the trip wasn't without its discomfort. Something about the roadway troubled Victor, something he couldn't put his finger on. It was the same feeling he had experienced while watching the film at the commissioner's briefing. Something was the matter, but *what?* Maybe it would come to him later . . . when he could afford the time to think about it. Later . . . after he took a look inside the building that stood so starkly reflected in the corrosive sodium glare.

There were only two gate panels in the Quonset hut and they both faced away from the roadway cul-de-sac, one in each end wall. Victor was thankful for that—it reduced his chances of detection. Easing his way up to one of the panels, his body flattened against the metal siding of the building, he kept his eyes peeled for guards. He saw none. "Now," he thought, "if only my luck can hold." He slid his hand along the panel divide until he located the gatelock. The small metal nub felt great between his fingers: it was a mesh-tumbler model, simple to pick. Simple for Victor. He set to his task with a fierce concentration, and in a matter of minutes the lockhinge disengaged and fell away. Ever so gently, Victor moved the panel a few inches apart and peered inside.

The first thing he saw were the pulverators. There was a whole row of them, mechanical behemoths more massive, more imposing than he would have believed had he not been staring at them with his own eyes. The second thing he saw were the five men sitting at a card table down at the opposite end of the building.

It seemed that luck was still on Victor's side. Had he tried to enter the building through the other gate panel, the men at the table would have spotted him immediately; as it turned out, however, he was able to slip inside without being seen, sliding the gate panels silently shut behind him.

It was not until Victor actually stood inside the Quonset hut that he could truly appreciate its immensity. Fully the size of two airplane hangars, it rose to a height of five stories at the center of its sloping ceiling. Yet even these expansive dimensions couldn't hide the prodigious size of the pulverators, squatting like four prehistoric beasts in the half shadows of the front wall. No tyrannosaurus, though, ever had the appetite of a pulverator. In one hour, a single machine could eat through a two-story office building or consume sixty automobiles—reducing 125 tons of brick or metal into fifty-pound packages of compressed refuse, neatly boxed and ready for recycling.

Looking up into the awesome bulk of the lead pulverator, Victor had no doubts about its destructive capacity. What he observed was a finely tooled, mobile wrecking factory which was part bulldozer, part baler, and part shark. Victor was most impressed by the lethal versatility built into the front of the machine. Huge hydraulic ramming plates could be locked into place, creating a battering ram capable of buckling concrete walls with a thrusting force of fifteen wrecking balls. Or these plates could be opened, revealing a blade-lined pulper capable of slashing and crushing tons of debris with herculean force. The pulper was fed with a power shovel or, in the case of large objects, by two steel mandibles attached to the sides of the pulverator. It was the kind of vehicle, Victor decided, that would fare well in a head-on collision. He gave the mechanical leviathan one final perusal and moved on. It was time to resume the search for clues to Mike Lin's behavior, and a likely place to look was down at the other end of the building.

"Pass."

"Pass."

"Bet a quarter."

"Call."

"Bump a quarter."

"I'll see it."

Victor could hear the voices clearly even before he could see the speakers. It was obvious that Mike Lin and his friends weren't high rollers, and Victor wondered how two-bit gamblers would respond to high-stakes pressure. He edged out a way on the narrow crossbeam that held him suspended some one hundred feet off the ground. Below, he could just see the edge of a tattered table. He inched out a bit further and was rewarded with an unobstructed view of seven men engrossed in a game of five-card stud.

It took Victor only a few seconds to observe each player and commit his face to memory. He wasn't surprised to spot Pete Torber at the table. He was seated next to Mike Lin and, judging from the number of chips stacked in front of him, was the game's big winner.

For fifteen minutes Victor remained uncomfortably in

place, hoping to hear something that might shed some
light on the Lin-Stevens meeting or the Stenley abduction. It was no use. If the men below knew anything, they
weren't talking. The only topic of conversation was poker
—penny-ante poker. Victor finally gave up in disgust.

It was on his way out of the Quonset hut that Victor
made his discovery—in a small room just a few hundred
feet from the poker table. He had noticed a shaft of light
spilling out from beneath the door, had tried the lock and
found it open. Cautiously he had eased the door ajar,
peeking through the tiny crack. A man was inside, seated
at some type of control panel. Victor had wanted to get a
closer look at the panel but couldn't risk it. The man at
the console or one of the card players might have spotted
him, particularly if he opened the door further and allowed additional light to filter out of the room. What he
had seen, however, convinced Victor that the panel was
a "sender," transmitting signals of some sort. But what
kind of signals? The question was certainly worth pursu-
ing further—and Victor made a mental note to do so . . .
if he got the chance.

A light rain was falling when Victor emerged from the
Quonset hut. It was a gentle rain, the kind that soothed
Victor and helped him think more clearly. Retracing his
steps along the paved roadway, he sifted through his
impressions of the Tork Wrecking Yard and tried to forge
some coherent conclusions from them. All he could come
up with were unanswered questions: Why had there
been such little security around the yard? What was the
purpose of the control panel in the Quonset hut? What
was there about the road he was on that was so trouble-
some? And, of course, what the hell was Mike Lin doing
with Nick Stevens? Victor still didn't know the answer to

that question. But he was beginning to get an idea of someone who might—and that someone was Gil Marba.

"Grrrrr . . ."

The sound stopped Victor in his tracks. This time he *had* heard something, and he knew where it came from. About a quarter mile away, just past the mounds of wrecked cars, a battered warehouse fronted the road. Quickening his pace, Victor veered off the pavement and circled the building in search of a way in. There was only one entrance and it was bolted shut with a maglock he couldn't pick. "Son of a bitch," he hissed, taking a deep breath. That's when he noticed the smell. He took another breath. The odor was so weak it was hard to identify, but it faintly resembled concussion gas. For an instant Victor wondered if possibly someone might be inside the building. Then he decided not. The sound he had heard was made by some kind of animal, not a human being. He was sure of that.

CHAPTER TEN

By the time Victor reached Marba's office, he knew what he had to do. Time was running out and he needed some answers badly—answers that only Marba could supply. Unfortunately, in seeking the answers he would have to confront Marba with the bitter realities concerning Stenley—realities that might push the fanatical old man over the edge. It was a chance he'd have to take.

"Slaughter," the anxious voice called out. It was Marba, motioning to Victor from a doorway across from his office. "In here."

Victor turned and walked past Marba into a large room filled with video monitors and transmitting equipment. "What the hell is all this?"

"Later," Marba barked impatiently, shutting the door loudly. "Where were you? You're a half hour late."

"My fault," Victor apologized, not wanting to do anything to provoke Marba further. "I've been running on four hours of sleep for the past two nights."

Marba pounded his fist into his hand. "Stenley's still missing and you're worried about sleep. Well, I haven't been in bed for three days, and you don't see me dragging my ass. What's the matter with you, anyway?" he fumed. "I thought they were supposed to teach you delta rehab at that fucking academy."

Victor raised his hands. "I'm sorry, I said."

"All right. Don't let it happen again." Marba walked

over to a transmission console and collapsed into a chair.

Victor had become accustomed to the old man's standard morning bluster, but this was something more. "Is
there anything else bothering you?" he asked, moving
over to join Marba at the console.

"You're damn right," he blurted. "Just let's drop it—
you wouldn't understand." Marba reached into his
pocket, pulled out a crumpled handkerchief and rubbed
it over his face. "Tell me what happened with Stevens."

Victor braced himself for an argument. "I have to ask
you a question first."

"What do you mean, 'ask me a question first'?" Marba
stopped wiping his face and began wrapping the handkerchief methodically around the knuckles of his right
hand. "I want to know about Stevens, and I want to know
now . . . right a—"

"Listen!" Victor's tone of voice stopped Marba in mid-
word. It was an angry, emphatic utterance, delivered
with a forcefulness that caught the old man off guard.
"I can solve this case for you," Victor claimed, taking advantage of Marba's momentary surprise to drive his point
home, ". . . but not unless I get your help in answering
my question."

Marba squeezed the handkerchief tighter around his
hand and glared at Victor.

"Just give me a few minutes—I think I'm onto something big."

"I don't believe you," Marba scoffed, his composure
returning. "You're stalling. What for? Did you blow the
Stevens job?"

"You know my Psycor profile. You know how many
cases I've solved." Victor softened his voice. "I'm only
asking for a few minutes."

Marba unwound his handkerchief from his hand and

jammed it into his pocket. "Okay," he said sullenly, "but you better not be wasting my time."

"I won't," Victor promised, "just tell me how the Dregs and the Council get along in this city."

"What the hell does that have to do with anything?"

"You said you'd answer . . ."

"It's a stupid question. How do you think they get along? How does a bloodsucker get along with its victim? You've been uptown; you know about the drug addiction and the protection rackets. Who do you think runs the show? And who do you think pays for it? In this town the Council takes and the Dreg gives: and when the Dreg decides he doesn't want to give, he's beaten or killed."

"Why don't the Dregs go to the police?"

"Now there's a good one," Marba snorted. "Like jumping from the frying pan into the fire. The cops hate the Dregs worse than the Council does—at least the Council needs the poor bastards around to turn a profit. The police could care less what happens to Dregs: they ignore them when they're in trouble and they kill them when they cause trouble."

"Why?"

"Because they're weak and sick and because people think they're to blame for New York's problems. Didn't you know," Marba joked bitterly, "they're all on welfare and they kill daily for drugs." He shook his head sadly. "You asked me what was bothering me when you came in this morning. You still want to know?"

"Yes."

"I saw two Dregs murdered in a police stakeout."

"Murdered?"

"Murdered. I'll show you." Marba reached over to the console control and activated a bank of rerun monitors.

"A camera at the stakeout recorded this footage early this morning," he explained, pointing to one screen. "What do you see?"

"The interior of a store—grocery store, probably."

"What else?"

"A clerk standing at a counter with two cops crouched down behind him."

"Okay, now watch every move those cops make from now on."

Victor stared at the monitor. The two officers weren't doing much of anything except looking uncomfortable in their bulky bulletproof vests. Then the front door of the shop burst open and they moved into action, drawing their ARC pistols and scurrying to opposite ends of the counter. In front of them a man with a gun was approaching the clerk, saying something which Victor lip-read as "Empty the cash drawer."

Then things seemed to explode. The employee ducked behind the counter at the same time the cops jumped up, their guns leveled at the intruder. Because their backs were to the camera, Victor couldn't tell if they said anything, but for a moment the gunman seemed to be listening. *Seemed* to be, but Victor would never be sure, for in the next instant an ARC blast caught the would-be robber just above the neck, pulperizing his face in a spray of cartilage and flesh.

"That's how the police treat Dregs," Marba concluded, switching off the monitor in disgust.

"The man was committing a crime, though," Victor pointed out.

"Yes . . . probably to get money for the Council."

"That doesn't change the fact that he was engaged in a felony."

"It was a setup . . . a turkey shoot," Marba argued, his

voice rising in anger again. "They didn't have to kill the guy. Wound him—maybe—but blow his head off? It was fucking cold-blooded murder, pure and simple."

Victor didn't press the issue further. "If the Dregs can't depend on the police, why don't they organize and fight the Council themselves?" he asked, trying to steer the conversation back to the original line of inquiry.

"Some have tried but it just hasn't worked. And you know why?" Marba looked at Victor as if he expected him to know the answer. "Because most of them are too fucking scared of organized crime to fight back. And who can blame them? It's not easy to fight guns with your bare hands. Not easy . . ." Marba's voice trailed off and for a few minutes his eyes glazed over with a faraway look. When he spoke again the tone was subdued. "That was the beauty of Stenley. People weren't scared anymore when they listened to her. She gave them a sense of pride, a sense of unity that made them want to stand together. She made them strong. That's why we need her back so badly."

"That explains your hunch about why the Council wanted her dead."

"Yes . . . they saw her as a threat because she could organize the Dregs. And that's the one thing they couldn't afford to let happen."

"What about your two friends Lin and Torber—the ones we're supposed to see today—have—"

"That meeting has been postponed till tomorrow," Marba broke in.

Victor brushed away the interruption. "Have they tried to organize the Dregs, too?"

A flicker of surprise passed over the lieutenant's face. "That's right. What made you think that?"

"Just a feeling," Victor replied, not wanting to reveal the real reason. "Have they been successful?"

"No. And I've been trying to discourage them. They're too much like you Psycor boys: they think violence can solve everything. Stenley's way is the best way—through the courts, and through the weight of public support."

"What's stopped them? The fear problem again?"

"That's right. What kind of protection can they guarantee someone after they tell him to buck the Council?"

Suddenly it hit Victor. One moment he was listening to Marba's reply and a moment later his mind was wandering back several hours, back to the paved road fronting the Quonset hut. And in a flash he knew what it was about the road that had bothered him: it was the stacks of wrecked cars lining both sides of the pavement. They had been practically devoid of dust, free of the copper-gray powder that seemed to lie like a blanket over everything else in the wrecking yard. Which meant they had been very recently moved to their position along the roadway.

"What's the matter?"

"Uh?" Victor shook his head and looked at Marba.

"I said, what's the matter?"

"Oh . . . nothing . . . I was just thinking, that's all."

"Well, you mind letting me in on it?"

"Yeah. Sure." Victor stood up and walked about, trying to dissipate some of the energy that had suddenly welled up inside him. He could sense that the kidnap puzzle was almost solved; that he was putting the last remaining pieces together in their appropriate pattern. "What do you think would happen if Lin and Torber decided to stand up to the Council and they were successful?"

"What's that? How?"

"Forget the technicalities," Victor said excitedly. "Let's

say they were able to make the Council lose face or, better yet, lose men—do you think that might convince the other Dregs to join them?"

"Who knows? . . . It might . . . but damnit, stop talking conjecture and tell me what the hell you're driving at."

Victor decided it was time to level with the old man. "Yesterday when I went to interrogate Stevens I spotted him talking with Mike Lin."

There was a stunned silence. "Mike Lin . . ." Marba mumbled the name in a tone of voice that was half questioning and half disbelieving.

"Mike Lin."

Victor could almost feel Marba's brain working, could imagine it running through all the possible reasons his Dreg friend would be consorting with a known criminal.

"Are you sure it was Lin?" he asked.

"You saw my profile analysis—you know I have a photographic memory."

"But Lin and Stevens . . ." he protested. "It just doesn't make any sense at all."

"It makes all the sense in the world if the Council still wants Stenley dead and Mike Lin still wants to organize the Dregs."

Marba got up from his chair, a bewildered expression on his face. "I don't see . . ."

"Of course you don't see," Victor broke in. "You don't *want* to see." He got a certain grim satisfaction from observing the old man in such a total state of befuddlement. "After I spotted Lin talking with Stevens, I followed him off the ship and uptown to a place called the Tork Wrecking Yard. He met there with Pete Torber and some other men I've never seen before."

"So, what's that supposed to prove?" Marba asked defensively. "Lin lives at the wrecking yard and so does Torber—Pete owns it."

Victor continued, undaunted. "I think they're planning to snare themselves a few Council members, using the wrecking yard as a trap."

Marba's expression changed from bewilderment to disdain. "That has to be the most incredible piece of bullshit I've ever heard."

"Why? You agreed it would help their cause if they could make the Council lose face. Just think . . ."

"Think . . . shit . . . *you* think. You think Lin and Torber are stupid? You think just because they're Dregs they don't have minds? Well, you think wrong, mister. They know when to fight and when not to—and they're certainly not going to challenge an army of armed hoodlums with what they've got: eight or nine men with not a gun between them."

"Wait a minute . . ."

"No, you wait." Marba was furious now, his hands clenched into tight fists. "What proof do you have that they're setting a trap, anyway?"

"The main roadway going into the yard, for one. It's been lined with wrecked cars to make turnoffs impossible and force traffic into the cul-de-sac fronting the main building."

"Some trap," Marba scoffed. "The Council has a mobile detachment of trained killers riding around in armored vans—five enforcers and ten attack dogs to a vehicle. One of those vans could wipe out your so-called roadblock and every Dreg in the area in a matter of minutes. And don't think Lin and Torber don't know it. Besides," Marba added, turning slightly to get a full view of Victor, "there's nothing that Lin or Torber have that would make the Council come to the wrecking yard in the first place."

"They have Helen Stenley."

Marba's head jerked up and his mouth snapped open. "What did you say?" He asked the question in a way that suggested Victor would be wise to reconsider his statement.

He didn't. "They have Stenley—she's the bait for the trap. The bait that Lin dangled in front of Stevens—the bait that's going to bring the Council to the wrecking yard."

Marba closed his eyes and massaged the lids with his fingers. After a while he spoke, gritting his teeth as if he wanted to crush each word as it came out of his mouth. "Are you telling me that two of my closest friends have kidnapped a woman who they love and respect to set up a battle they can't possibly win?"

"Not exactly. I never said they couldn't win the battle and I never said they kidnapped Stenley. My contention is that Stenley was in on the abduction from the beginning."

"That's enough." Marba stepped in front of Victor, an ugly look on his face. "Don't you ever talk to me about Stenley like that again. Never."

Victor didn't budge an inch. "What is the matter with you?" he complained, his patience wearing thin. "The woman isn't some fucking saint—she's just another true believer who thinks it's all right to bend the law to bolster her cause. If you don't believe what I say, why don't you go uptown and check out Lin and Torber yourself?"

"You bet I will—them and Stevens and that hit man, too. You're going to wish you never said what you did about Stenley when I get finished destroying your stupid little theory. Right now you tell me where I can see Stevens and his hit man."

"I'm afraid it won't be possible for you to talk with the hit man," Victor said matter-of-factly.

"What do you mean, 'not possible'?" Marba put one hand firmly on Victor's shoulder. "Where is he?"

"Dead."

Marba sagged like a jackhammer had caught him in the belly. "Dead?" He asked the question as if he didn't believe it. "Don't tell me you killed him?"

"I had to—he could've been big trouble."

"Oh, my God." Marba mouthed the words slowly, shaking his head from side to side. "You really did murder the guy, didn't you? After all I told you—after everything the regional office told you—you just went right out and did it your own way anyway." The words were coming faster now, at a higher pitch. Victor could sense the rage building in Marba, could feel it like some white-hot energy flowing from the old man's hand into his own shoulder. Too late, he started to brace himself.

"Asshole!" The word exploded from Marba's lips at the same time his free hand exploded from his side, catching Victor flush on the cheek and spinning him violently against his chair. "Rotten punk son of a bitch!" he cursed, giving Victor a brutal kick in the thigh as he stumbled to the floor. "I'll have your fucking head for this," he shouted, taking a second swipe at Victor as he scrambled out of the way.

Victor wasn't used to making mistakes. Mistakes in his line of work cost lives. Yet he had made two costly errors with Marba—he had underestimated the lieutenant's anger over the killing, and his physical strength—and now he was paying dearly for it. Staggering to his feet, he prepared himself as best he could for the expected deluge of blows and counterblows. They never came. As suddenly as Marba's violence erupted, it subsided, and he stepped away from Victor, his body rigid, his hands working aimlessly up the front of his shirt. "I hit you . . . an officer should never do that," he said apologetically, stooping over to pick up Victor's overturned chair. "A human being should never do that. But you don't make it very easy for a person to be human—you know that?"

Victor rubbed the swelling right side of his face, saying nothing.

"You *do* know that, don't you?"

Victor seemed to look right through Marba. "I know that you're an old man. And you know it, too."

Marba's expression softened. "I suppose you're right," he admitted, pausing. "But at least I'm not a hollow man."

"You're hollow-headed—you and that Stenley woman and anyone else who wants to save this stinking city."

"The people who want to save this city have more brains and guts than you'll ever have. And values. God, if only Psycor had taught you a set of values." Marba straightened his jacket and walked toward the door.

"Where are you going?" Victor called after him.

"Back to my office . . . back to work."

"What about what I just told you?"

"I'm going to forget you ever told me that bullshit. And you're going to forget I ever lost my temper with you. We'll call it even. Go follow up on that Stevens interrogation and let me know when you uncover some real leads." Marba stopped at the door and turned. "I don't expect you to understand this, but for a while there yesterday I thought you might turn out different from the rest of those Psycor butchers. A little more humane, maybe. You disappointed me, Slaughter, you really did."

"I'm doing what I have to to accomplish my mission,"

Victor replied guiltlessly. "Your ways don't work—not now, not in New York. Unethical people don't play by your ethical rules—they take what they want and you're not going to stop them with fucking appeals to decency and moral behavior."

Marba opened the door. "I'm sorry for you," he said.

"Just a minute," Victor called out. It was no use. Marba stepped out and shut the door behind him, leaving Victor alone to contemplate what he should do next.

CHAPTER ELEVEN

It was after 1 P.M. by the time Victor finally got a chance to speak with Marty. She sat beside him on the tour bus, a stoic look on her face. "I just received a directive from Central Operations," she said.

"About Marba?"

"Yes. Terminate him."

Victor didn't try to hide his surprise. "That simple, eh? After all those years of service."

"What's the problem now?" she grumbled, obviously annoyed. "The last time I saw you you were begging me to get rid of him."

"Get him off the case . . . not kill him."

"Are you challenging a directive?"

Victor glowered at his regional director. "Don't get raggy with me—you know I'll do it. I just think it's a pretty severe decision."

"But necessary. After you called this morning we took your advice and put a tail on Marba. He left his office about an hour after you did—in an extremely agitated state, according to the field report."

Victor snapped his fingers. "I knew he was lying when he told me he'd be staying in his office." He looked at Marty critically. "Why wasn't I informed of this earlier?"

"We didn't think there was any reason to. We followed him to the Guild Building and waited for him to make his next move."

"The Guild Building? The Council maintains a suite there."

"We know."

"And he's still there?"

"No."

"Where is he?"

"That's the trouble: we don't know."

"You don't know?"

"He slipped out of the building somehow without being spotted."

"Oh, that's just what I needed. He probably knew he was being tailed."

"We're not sure of that, either."

"Damn! What the hell are you sure of?" Victor checked his watch. "He's probably headed uptown right now. Can't your office do anything right?"

"It was a slipup," Marty countered, her eyes flashing. "It could happen to anyone."

"It wouldn't happen to me."

"Just forget it," she said sternly. "It was a mistake, and it's done. Right now we've got a much bigger problem. When we went back to the police department to see if Marba was there, we discovered a 20-Range ARC pistol was missing."

"That's an experimental weapon."

"Marba has it. We're checking now to see how he got it out of the lab."

Victor rubbed his hands down the sides of his face. "That changes the whole ball game," he said. "That gun can pulp a tank."

"Or vaporize the person using it. The model he took has no safety casing over the compression chamber."

"Would he know that?"

"Probably. The chamber and casing design on the 20-Range is similar to standard models."

"What about detonating the chamber?"

"Same as on the standard models, except the 20-Range has an arrow indicator. When the chamber is twisted to the detonate position the arrow points straight up." Marty took a deep drag on the cigarette she was smoking and brushed the accumulated ashes into the ashtray on her armrest. "Once the chamber is twisted to detonate, it'll explode in ten minutes unless it's moved back to its original position, at which point the ten-minute cycle starts over."

Victor drummed his fingers against his knee. "What's the kill range if the compression chamber ruptures?"

"Hard to say."

"There's gotta be some kind of estimate. What the hell are they doing over in munitions anyway—sleeping in their own concussion gas?"

"They exploded a type-20 a few weeks ago at Desert Flats. It vaporized a monkey fifty feet from ground zero —and that was in the open. In an enclosed space the effects of the detonation would be even greater."

"That powerful, eh?"

"There was nothing left—not even a fragment of bone."

"Let's hope Marba doesn't rupture in public," Victor wisecracked.

"That's not funny." Marty crushed out her cigarette and pushed the recliner button on her seat arm. "Do you think you can find him?"

"Yes."

"And the Stenley woman?"

"What happens if I don't?"

"A lot of important people are going to be very unhappy. Washington people—they're getting real heat from the public on this one. They've already told us to crack down on the Council and anyone else who might know where she is."

"I'll find 'er."

"When will I get an update?"

"Tonight—after I check out a hunch."

Marty toyed with a large amethyst bracelet on her left hand. "You don't believe in sharing information, do you?"

"I believe in working alone—and that includes keeping my plans to myself. I stay alive that way."

"Have it your own way," she shrugged, stretching out in her seat and closing her eyes, "as long as you get the job done."

Victor wanted to get some rest, too. Reclining in his window seat, he tried to lull himself to sleep by counting the boarded brownstones and tinned storefronts of Greenwich Village as they passed by in unbroken monotony. It was no use. Thoughts of Marba kept intruding into his consciousness, thoughts of what he had to do to the old man. It angered Victor that he couldn't get the termination off his mind. He knew that Marba's sentence of death was justified, yet he felt uneasy about being the executioner. It was a bad sign, a very bad sign. There was no room for doubt or indecisiveness in a termination assignment and he knew it—not when a split second might mean the difference between the success and failure of the mission.

Victor tapped Marty on the shoulder.

"What is it?" she mumbled, opening her eyes reluctantly.

"Something's bothering me about Marba."

Marty stretched her arms out in front of her and sat upright in her seat. "What?"

"His demotion to the Fourth Division. Was it really a case of insubordination?"

"According to the police or Marba?"

"Whoever was right."

"That's not easy to say. . . ."

"Then tell me your opinion."

"Why do you want to know, anyway?"

"Just curious."

Marty turned her head to look at Victor, a suspicious expression on her face.

"I'd really like to know," Victor assured her.

"All right," she agreed. "It was his opposition to URDEC that started it."

"Urban Decentralization?"

"Yes. He thought it was all a big-business smokescreen —an excuse to leave the city when the going got rough. And he said so."

"That mustn't have gone over too well with the Manhattan moneymen."

"It didn't. And things got worse after he blamed URDEC for the declining interest in urban problems."

"What was the connection?"

"He felt that once everything of value was safely moved outside the city, nobody gave a damn about what was left behind—the poor, the infirm, the addicts. They weren't a threat anymore."

"Do you think he was right?"

"Not totally—but it was true that with URDEC there was an increasing tendency for the police to ignore the Dregs and their problems."

"Which enraged Marba."

"It did—that's what led to his demotion. He was a

precinct captain at the time. When he heard there was an unofficial police policy to stay outside the Dreg Zones, he went to the commissioner and said the department had the responsibility to preserve law and order in the slums and that he was going to send men in to get the job done."

"He never was one to keep his thoughts to himself. What did the commissioner say?"

" 'No,' politely."

"Then . . . ?"

"Marba asked him again."

"And he probably replied 'no,' not so politely."

"Correct. So Marba just went ahead and ordered some men from his precinct to go in, anyway."

"Which the commissioner didn't appreciate."

"That's an understatement! He called Marba in and told him what a splendid job he'd do in the Records Division. They couldn't bust him because that would've meant a hearing and publicity—and the commissioner's office didn't want publicity on anything concerning the treatment of Dregs. Nobody did."

"So they buried him instead. And he just let them do it?"

"Yes."

"But why? It doesn't sound like Marba."

"I asked him the same question."

"What did he say?"

"He said he had a job to finish."

"That's it?"

"That's all he said. He didn't even appeal to Psycor to intervene on his behalf."

Victor thought about that for a moment. "Maybe it was better he didn't," he said. "Maybe it was better he didn't."

CHAPTER TWELVE

Bernie Richter was feeling good. It was a crisp Thursday afternoon, traffic was light, and he was on his way to a killing. Turning off Broadway onto Amsterdam, he checked in his side mirror to make sure the rest of the convoy was following in proper formation behind his Van-guard. It was his most important assignment as Van Commander and there was no way he was going to foul it up. Not after ten years as a professional terminator with seventy-nine kills to his credit. And certainly not after the First Councilman had told him that it would be the most important hit he ever made.

"Hey, Bernie."

Richter turned to his radioman.

"You wanna give the scramble instructions? We're getting pretty close."

"Yeah. Turn on the mike."

The radioman buzzed intervehicle alert and activated the microphone in the center of the van's steering wheel. "You're on two way, go ahead," he signaled.

Richter checked up and down the roadway carefully before he began transmitting. There wasn't a car within two blocks of him, nor, for that matter, any pedestrians—they had long since ducked under cover. It gave Richter a feeling of power to move unchallenged through upper Manhattan—tacitly ignored by the police and fearfully avoided by the Dregs. "This is Van-guard control, signal if you read me," he said.

Four red lights appeared almost simultaneously on the transmitter outboard. "Everyone's receiving," the radio-man told Richter.

"All right," Richter began, keeping his eyes focused on the windshield as he talked, "I want a final equipment run-through. Van two, report."

There was a momentary silence and then a voice crackled over the Van-guard receiverset. "Five men, five pistols, two shotguns, fifteen grenades, and ten dogs—all checked and operational."

"Van three . . ."

"Five men, five machine guns, fifteen grenades, and ten dogs—all checked and operational."

"Van four . . ."

"Five men, two CG launchers, two flamethrowers, five pistols, and ten dogs—all checked and operational."

"Hold it, Van four." Richter went through his mental list of equipment. "You were issued three concussion-gas launchers."

"Sorry, Bernie, Pignocchi down at loading was supposed to tell you one launcher was busted."

"Well, he never did." Richter turned to Carl Sulzer, his second in command. "You get on that Pignocchi when we get back, you understand?"

"Sure, Bernie—don't worry—I'll take care of it."

"You do that." Richter shook his head in disgust. "All right, Van five, report."

"Five men, five machine guns, fifteen grenades, and ten dogs—all checked and operational."

Richter turned to Sulzer again. "Report for Van-guard one."

Sulzer leaned over so he was closer to the steering

wheel microphone. "Four men, three pistols, one ARC gun, nine grenades—all checked and operational."

"Okay. Equipment reports confirmed." Richter passed Ninety-sixth Street and began to decelerate the Vanguard. "Now here are your orders," he barked. "One of our Dreg informers tipped us that Helen Stenley is being held by some of his friends in the Tork Wrecking Yard. She must be found, terminated, and her body left on the premises so the Dregs will be implicated in her kidnapping. And no slipups. You hear that, you guys in four?"

"Gotcha, Bernie," came the immediate response from the fourth van.

"Good. You make sure Danny and Frank go mellow on those flamethrowers. I don't want Stenley charred to a crisp. The body has to be left in identifiable condition—you get me?"

"It's done, Bernie."

"Well, it better be," he growled ominously. "Now all of you listen—we've got one other little job to do. The Dregs who kidnapped Stenley: I want them dead, every fucking one of them. And not just nice dead—I want them mutilated, I want them burned, I want them torn to pieces by the dogs. I want those bodies to be a fitting reminder to the rest of the fucking Dreg scum who might be thinking about going up against the Council. Is that clear?"

There was a silence.

"Is that clear, damnit!?"

Red lights began popping all over the transmitter outboard.

"That's better." Richter paused for a moment to let his orders sink in before he continued. "Now this is going to be an easy job—a setup. The only reason we're bringing in five vans and arming you to the teeth is for a show of strength. There'll be Dregs all over the area who'll be watching what goes on in that wrecking yard—so you better damn well give them a good show. I want every bit of ammunition used. I want every dog turned loose. And most of all, I want to see every one of you hustle out there like you've never hustled before. I'll personally cut the balls off any man who drags his ass on this assignment. You get what I'm saying?"

The transmitter outboard lighted up again.

Richter seemed satisfied. "All right," he said, "we'll be going in a few blocks from here. Keep in formation, and stand by for skirmish instructions." Then he turned to his radioman. "Keep all channels clear," he directed, "but flip off my mike for now."

The radioman did as he was told.

Up ahead, Richter could see the entrance to the Tork Wrecking Yard. He cut his speed even further and edged along slowly, reflexively looking for signs of trouble he knew he wouldn't find. "Listen," he said to the three men riding with him, "I want to tell you I met with the First Councilman this morning and he told me that if we didn't come up with Stenley's body somebody might come up with ours."

"Hey, what's the big deal with making sure her corpse is found in the wrecking yard anyway?" Sulzer asked. "What's to stop people from saying we planted it there?"

"Sulzer, did anybody ever tell you why you didn't get my job? Because you're an idiot. You don't think with your brain." Richter leaned over and gave his second in command a cuff on the ear. "Once the body is found there it won't make any difference. The public stink will die down and the police will stop leaning on us. But until we can produce Stenley, we're going to get heat—and the Council doesn't like heat. You follow, Sulzer?"

"Yeah, Bernie—I didn't mean nothing by it."

"That's fine. You just do the killing and let me do the thinking." Richter boxed Sulzer on the ear again. "Now take a look at that aerial photomap on your lap and double-check me to the skirmish point."

Richter swung the Van-guard smoothly off Columbus Avenue onto the paved roadway that snaked into the center of the wrecking yard.

"Just stay on this road—it'll lead right to the front of the Quonset hut," Sulzer instructed, using his index finger to trace the path the Van-guard was traveling.

"I'm with you," Richter replied, keeping his speed at a steady ten miles per hour so that the other vans could follow comfortably in close formation. "I think I see it already, about two blocks beyond those piles of wrecked cars."

"What cars?" Sulzer looked at the map and then at the two mounds of cars that lined the roadway a few hundred yards ahead. "That's funny," he said, puzzled, "those cars aren't on this picture at all."

"Here, let me see that." Richter reached over and snatched the map from Sulzer's hands. "You're right," he agreed, looking twice at the photomap. "When was this taken?"

"A week ago," Lanning, the first gunner, answered.

"Very interesting." Richter's lips parted in an ugly sneer. "I think our little junkyard friends are planning an ambush." He stepped down on the gas pedal ever so slightly. "I'm starting to enjoy this job more every minute."

From his vantage point atop the Quonset hut, Victor could see the five vans approaching along the narrow roadway below. It gave him a sense of satisfaction to see proof that he was right about Lin and Stevens—that the confrontation he had predicted between Council and Dregs was about to commence. It also pleased him that he had arrived in time to observe the clash because, if he was right again, once the fighting was over the Dregs would lead him to where they had Stenley hidden. The only problem was whether there'd be any of them left to follow after the combat ended. Victor wondered if the Dregs had anticipated such a massive show of force by their foe. Watching the five bulky vehicles edging forward, their three-inch armor hulls reflecting metal-gray against the overcast sky, he started to suspect that the Dregs had made a serious mistake in trying to ambush the Council.

Bernie Richter felt the same way. Reaching the roadway cul-de-sac, he ordered his convoy into a V-form skirmish line and prepared to wipe out the Dreg resistance with one awesome, sweeping assault. For a moment he waited, his Van-guard poised at the center of the attack formation like the tip of an arrow ready to pierce the front wall of the Quonset hut not more than twenty feet away. And in that moment he heard the crashing sound behind him. "What the hell . . ." he swore, angry that his concentration had been disturbed. "What was that?"

Lanning was the first person to discover the answer. Squinting through a rear gun turret, he spotted the swirl of dust rising from the roadway some two hundred feet away. "Shit, there must be ten cars blocking the road back there."

Richter spun out of his seat. "Out of the way," he ordered, pushing aside his first gunner and peering through the turret. "Wiseass fuckers," he exclaimed, staring through the opening for a few moments longer.

"What is it?" Sulzer asked.

"Those little bastards are trying to hem us in," he replied, sounding like a man suddenly confronted by a pesky mosquito. Richter turned away from the turret and scrambled back to his seat. "I'm gonna mash their heads right up their asses," he promised, buckling into his body harness. "You men, strap yourselves in—I'm gonna take this van right through that fucking wall. Bronski, put me on intervan."

Bronski jabbed the mike control button on the transmitter outboard. "Go," he said, pointing to his commander.

"All vans, this is Richter. The Dregs put a block on our tail, but forget it—we'll bust it on our way out. Right now we're going in—and I don't want anything alive when we leave. Our informer told us the Dregs are in the Quonset, so let's get 'em before they spread out. They probably figure us for coming in the end doors, so we're going to take them through the wall. Vans two and three, I want you to follow me straight into the building and scramble at once. Vans four and five, lay back outside, but as soon as we're through the wall, scramble your forces and follow on foot. I want full firepower and I want it fast, is that clear?"

Bronski watched the pattern of lights appear on his outboard. "Full response, Bernie."

Richter glanced over at the transmitter to double-check his radioman's report. "All right. Lanning, we set on the ramming shield?"

"Engaged and ready."

"Then let's get this thing moving." Richter pulled the floor clutch into four-wheel drive and jammed the tri-throttle to full power. The engine roared to life, shaking the whole van as it built toward thrust force. Richter let the pressure intensify until the vehicle seemed ready to strip away the brakelocks that held it in place. Then he closed his hand over the catapult release lever and began to pull forward. "Check your harnesses," he warned, "here we go."

There was a tremendous roar and the Van-guard hurtled forward like a rock from a sling, its stubby steel-glas nose ready to break through the corrugated metal wall of the Quonset hut. It was in that first instant of acceleration that Bernie Richter knew something was terribly wrong. Instinctively he jammed on his brakes, but they were useless against such powerful momentum. There was nothing left to do but brace for the concussion, and Bernie Richter rocked forward, thrusting his head between his knees. Ten seconds later he was dead.

From his elevated vantage point, Victor witnessed the destruction of the Van-guard with a sense of admiration. The Dregs had produced an elegant extermination, full of surprise and precise timing. One moment the Van-guard was careening toward a harmless-looking wall and then . . . in the next instant . . . the wall caved out and four pulverators burst into view. The lead pulverator hit the Van-guard head on, shattering the front of the armored van with one thrust of its hydraulic ramming plates. Then it scooped up the disabled vehicle with its power shovel and tossed it into the teeth of the pulper. There was a rasping, crunching sound as the blades shredded the van and the hydropress crushed it into a small metal bolus. Then, as if it had never existed, the van was gone—its remains pushed down the throat of the pulverator to be digested and eventually excreted as a pure metal alloy.

George Gilder commanded Van two. In case of Van-guard destruction he knew he was to assume immediate responsibility for mission coordination; yet, as he watched Richter's vehicle disappear into the jaws of the pulverator, leadership duties were not his concern. Survival was—self-survival. Jamming the wheels of his van hard to the left, he swerved violently narrowly missing the steel mandibles of one pulverator and brushing by the ramming plates of another. That's when his luck ran out. Still skidding out of control, he slammed broadside into Van four as it cut across his path in blind retreat from the pulverator that had consumed Van-guard.

The impact of the collision seemed to clear George Gilder's mind. It was like he was back playing football, and the nervousness would go out of him when he made contact on the first play of the game. He grabbed his intervan mike, hoping it was still working. "This is Gilder," he said, his voice surprisingly calm. "Abandon your vehicles at once and commence ground skirmish. I repeat: abandon your vehicles immediately and commence ground skirmish." He tossed away the mike and yanked apart his safety harness. "Let's go," he shouted to the men in the van, pressing the panel release button on the dashboard control terminal. "Get the lead out! Scramble!"

It took twelve seconds to evacuate Van two. Gilder and his men needed every one of them. The last German shepherd had barely jumped clear of the vehicle when a pulverator came up behind the van, squeezed it like an accordion between its huge mandibles, and tossed it, crumpled and skewered, into the spinning blades of the pulper.

The men in Van four weren't as fortunate. Unable to operate their panel door, which was jammed shut from the collision with Gilder's van, they had to attempt escape through a narrow emergency exit in the back of their vehicle. Two crewmen made it out the small opening and the van's commander was halfway through when a pulverator bashed into the rear of the crippled vehicle. The impact buckled the back of the van, plugging up the escape hatch with twisted metal and the crushed body of the commander. Then, almost leisurely, the giant machine backed off, lowered its power shovel, and scooped the mangled van into the waiting pulper.

Peering down at the scene unfolding before him, Victor could recall only one other time he had witnessed such bedlam: in Spain during the run of the bulls. Only this time the bulls were mechanical beasts with steel-point horns, and the people they were chasing were paid killers armed with guns and grenades.

For a while it looked like the Dregs would rout their foes with ease. The pulverators roamed at will among the scattered Council forces, crushing shepherds and gunmen along the way and consuming the two remaining vans with gusto.

Then the tide of battle began to turn. The Council forces started to regroup and attack the pulverators in a coordinated manner, knocking out two of them with grenades and machine-gun fire. As powerful as the behemoths were, they were cumbersome and vulnerable to hit-and-run attacks—the kind of assaults they were now facing. A third pulverator spun out of control as its operator caught a burst of machine-gun bullets across the chest, and Victor could see the Dreg offensive collapsing. He sensed that once the Council forces got past the pulverators, there was nothing left to stop them from finishing off the Dregs inside the Quonset hut.

Or was there? Victor heard the sound before he saw anything. A chilling, howling sound—a sound he had heard once before. Then he spotted them: dogs, literally hundreds of them, pouring through a makeshift conduit opening onto the roadway from beneath the wrecked-car blockade. And in a flash he understood. The growling sound he had heard the night before, the concussion gas he had smelled—they both made sense now; they both pointed to the same conclusion: The Dregs had been trapping wild dogs and gassing them so that they could be roused and used if needed.

The Dregs certainly needed them now. Streaming down the road, angry, hungry, and maddened by the scent of German shepherds—they burst into the cul-de-sac, fur standing and fangs bared. Under normal conditions a wild dog wouldn't stand a chance fighting against an attack dog. Such was the case in the Tork Wrecking Yard, except that the wild dogs outnumbered trained German shepherds five to one.

They came in waves, the mangy, fierce-eyed mutts—and they were met with bullets and shepherds. They staggered and fell, and still they came. And when they fell a final time, new waves of beasts replaced them—ripping and clawing their way into whatever confronted them, dying with hunks of flesh clamped tightly between their teeth.

Victor estimated that there were some fifty wild dogs still on their feet when the remaining Council killers broke ranks and stumbled down the roadway toward the conduit and possible freedom. There were seven of them left, bruised and beaten men lurching desperately on—drawn by the slim hope of the conduit ahead and driven by the fear of the crazed dogs behind. Victor felt sorry for the men because he now realized what was going to happen to them. The Dregs had left nothing to chance. The small room Victor had spotted near the card table in the Quonset hut had a purpose. So did the man sitting at the "sender" panel—and Victor fully understood what was going to be "sent" over that transmitter.

The men were almost to the mouth of the conduit now. Victor could still see them clearly, running more rapidly as they realized that they could beat the dogs to the circular opening. The first man to reach the conduit dived headlong into the four-foot-high metal tube and scrambled forward on his belly. The others followed in close order, until all seven were inside the darkened passageway.

For a moment Victor wondered if the dogs would try to follow their human quarry into the duct, but he knew the question was academic. They'd never get the chance. In his mind's eye Victor could see the man in the small room pulling the lever forward on his "sender" panel. He focused his attention on the mouth of the conduit. One, maybe two seconds passed. Then there was a tremendous explosion and the entire blockade dissolved in a flash of fire and debris.

Observing the carnage strewn over the wrecking yard, Victor couldn't help but be amused. Marba had been right: the Dregs didn't have guns. But they did have dogs, dynamite, and pulverators—and in less than ten minutes they had annihilated the Council's mobile strike force. All in all, he had to admit, not a great day for organized crime.

Out in front of the Quonset hut, the one undamaged pulverator was sweeping back and forth across the cul-de-sac, raking up dead bodies and dog carcasses like so many leaves off the grass. Victor watched the work progress, realizing that in a very short time there would be no evidence of the battle left at all.

That's when he spotted Helen Stenley. She was walking toward the shattered front wall of the Quonset hut, flanked on either side by two Dregs Victor remembered seeing in the card game the night before. He scuttled along the edge of the roofway, watching them until he was sure they had disappeared inside. Then he entered the building, too—shimmying his way down from the roof along a metal girder and onto a section of elevated crossbeam that extruded where a portion of wall had been torn away.

As soon as Victor's eyes adjusted to the darker interior of the building, he recognized where he was. Below him he could see the tattered card table where Torber had been winning at poker the night before. Torber was there now, sitting across from Lin and Stenley and the two Dregs who had brought her in. Victor couldn't quite hear what they were saying so he edged forward along the crossbeam, pressing himself flat against the metal surface so that he couldn't be easily seen from the ground. Easing himself along a few feet at a time, he soon reached a suitable listening distance and could clearly hear Mike Lin telling Stenley how she had been used as bait to lure the Council to the wrecking yard.

She didn't like it one bit. "You had no right to do that," she complained. "I'm sick of your killing."

Lin glared at her sternly. "Don't you forget who planned the whole kidnap idea in the first place."

"That was to arouse public sympathy—and there was to be no violence. I told you that . . . no violence."

"You don't tell us anything, lady," Lin snapped.

Torber leaned over the table. "That's enough," he cautioned, putting a restraining hand on Lin's shoulder. "Right now we've got to get out of here and lay low awhile—the Council's sure to come up here with more men when they find out what happened."

"Exactly," Stenley interjected. "There's just going to be more bloodshed—you've accomplished nothing."

"No, that's where you're wrong," Torber replied gently. "What happened here today was a starting point for Dreg unity—a point to build from. Today we learned we could stand up to the Council and win—and we're not going to forget it. Neither will the rest of the Dregs in this city. We'll have our strength in numbers now, that I can promise you."

"Well, I want no part of it," Stenley objected. "I want to be released now . . . this instant."

"I'm afraid that won't be possible," Torber replied sadly.

Stenley didn't try to hide the fear in her face. "Look," she said, "if you're worried I'm going to say anything about all this—forget it. I won't say anything, I promise."

Torber's voice remained gentle. "That's not the problem. It's a matter of your value. As long as you stay missing, our cause is helped. We get more public sympathy, more chance for federal aid and, most important, the police are forced to crack down on the Council—keeping them busy while we grow stronger and consolidate our gains."

"But I don't want to stay," Stenley pleaded, starting to cry.

"I'm sorry." Torber walked over to Stenley and motioned for her to get up. "We just can't afford for you to be found; the future of the movement depends on it."

"So does the future of New York."

The voice caught everyone but Victor by surprise. Victor had been expecting Marba.

"The man *is* right, you know," Marba continued, stepping out from the shadows along the back wall, the experimental ARC pistol gripped firmly in his right hand. "Torber is always right, aren't you, Torber?" Marba pointed his gun directly at Torber's head. "Why don't you tell me how right you are—you with the big brains. I'll bet you planned the little show outside, didn't you?"

As Marba moved closer to the table, Victor spotted one of the Dregs moving his left hand slowly into his pants pocket.

Marba spotted him too, and fired one short burst from his ARC gun. Victor had never seen a 20-Range model fired before, and he was suitably impressed with the results. The brightness of the discharge alone almost blinded him, but that was nothing compared to what it did to the Dreg. It simply blew him into a thousand pieces, almost as if he were a drop of mercury struck by a hammer.

"Don't anybody else try something that foolish," Marba suggested, walking to within six feet of Stenley before he stopped. "You really let me down," he said ruefully, looking directly into the woman's eyes.

She turned away.

"The rest of you let me down, too. I thought you had some principles—I thought you were real New Yorkers." Marba's face clouded over with anger. "Well, I thought wrong. Now get up . . . move!"

"Wait a minute," Mike Lin protested. "We diced the fucking Council, what more do you want?"

Without warning, Marba stepped forward and smashed Lin across the forehead with the butt of his pistol. The force of the blow spun the Dreg out of his chair and sent him crashing to the floor, dazed and bleeding.

"Now move!" Marba shouted, jamming the muzzle of his gun against the side of Lin's head. So great was his rage that he didn't notice the shadowy figure descending from the crossbeams to the earthen floor below. Neither did anyone else. They were too concerned with the ARC pistol pointed at Lin's temple, too worried that Marba might pull the trigger.

Lin was more worried than anybody. Still groggy, he tried to obey Marba's directive. "I'm getting up . . ." he moaned, wiping the blood from his eyes and staggering to his feet. No sooner had he righted himself than Marba shoved him roughly forward, almost tumbling him to the ground again.

"Now all of you . . . get going!" he roared, waving his pistol toward the far end of the Quonset hut. This time there was no resistance to his order, and the four captives began moving uneasily through the building. They were almost to the end-door gate panel when Marba instructed them to stop beside a cinderblock saltshed. The shed door was partially closed and Marba momentarily turned away from his captives to kick it open.

That's when Victor made his move. Having trailed Marba across the Quonset hut, he now stood a scant fifteen feet from the old man, partially shielded from view by the metal ribbing that extended out from the side of the far wall. "Drop your gun, Marba," he commanded, his voice steely clear.

If Marba was startled by Victor's presence he didn't show it. He started to turn away from the saltshed as if nothing had happened.

"Don't even think it," Victor warned, tightening the grip on his ARC gun. "I can cut you down before you get halfway around."

Marba stopped moving. "What's the trouble?" he asked.

"Just drop the gun and then we'll talk."

"I don't understand—these four are under arrest and I'm taking them in."

"I said, drop the gun."

For a fraction of a second Marba's gun hand tensed, then relaxed. "All right," he agreed, "I'm putting it down

—but you better know I'm going to bust you right out of Psycor for this."

Marba dropped his weapon on the ground.

"Now kick it away from you."

"I'm not—"

"Kick it!"

Marba took a halfhearted swipe at the gun with the side of his foot, sending it skittering along the ground some five or six feet.

"Fine." Victor stepped away from the wall and scooped up the experimental weapon with his left hand. "Now move around slowly with your hands locked in front of you."

Marba turned around. As he did, Victor glanced down at the gun in his left hand. The small red arrow seemed to jump out at him, brash and straight up, twelve o'clock high. He gripped the cylinder as quickly as he could, twisting it back to its deactive position. Then he refocused his attention on Marba.

For a while Victor just stared at the old man, stared at his expression and tried to understand what depth of despair could cause a face to die like that. "You know why I'm here, don't you?" he said finally.

The old man said nothing.

"It's a job—I do what I'm told."

There was no response.

"Damn you!" Victor cursed. "What do you want me to do? I know what you have planned for those people over there. It won't make any difference. Can't you see that? New York is dead—give it up."

Marba remained silent, his eyes fixed on the gun in Victor's hand.

"You're not going to, are you? You'll die believing . . ." Victor let his voice trail off in midsentence. What the hell is the matter? he thought to himself. He had been assigned to kill—why wasn't he killing? He remembered Byer's class, thought back to the dogs in the ovens, back to the professor's words: "You kill quickly and cleanly . . . swiftly—with no mess." What was the purpose of all that training? To stand flatfooted in a shattered Quonset hut debating over the life of one worthless old man?

Victor raised the 20-Range ARC pistol and aimed for a heart shot. He had seen what the gun could do—death would certainly be swift and clean. A decade of Psycor experience helped curl his finger around the trigger, helped hold his hand steady while he readied a shot. Yet, try as he might, he couldn't fire his weapon. Right then Victor Slaughter realized he was no longer fighting Marba; he was fighting himself.

Turning the gun on its side, Victor twisted the compression chamber back to the detonate position and handed it to Marba. The two men looked at each other and they both understood. Victor left then, thinking about an old man dying an elegant death in a city he loved.